ADRIFT

The ship was going to pass them.

"Hey!" Flynn yelled. "Help!" He jumped to his feet to scream at the ship with what was left of his voice, to dance on the crate, to do anything at all to make someone on that ship see him. But the crate wasn't big enough to tolerate any violent movement. It tilted as Flynn leapt up, slewed as he sought his balance, and bucketed under his weight. Flynn hurtled into the sea.

Sally clutched the top of the pitching crate. She began to bawl from fright and pain, then she stopped and bit her lip. An immense shadow was passing slowly under the crate.

"A swift-paced survival adventure that'll hold readers to the end."   —*Kirkus Reviews*

Also by Allan Baillie

Little Brother

ADRIFT

ALLAN BAILLIE

PUFFIN BOOKS

PUFFIN BOOKS

Published by the Penguin Group

Penguin Books USA Inc., 375 Hudson Street, New York, New York 10014, U.S.A.

Penguin Books Ltd, 27 Wrights Lane, London W8 5TZ, England

Penguin Books Australia Ltd, Ringwood, Victoria, Australia

Penguin Books Canada Ltd, 10 Alcorn Avenue, Toronto, Ontario, Canada M4V 3B2

Penguin Books (N.Z.) Ltd, 182-190 Wairau Road, Auckland 10, New Zealand

Penguin Books Ltd, Registered Offices: Harmondsworth, Middlesex, England

First published in Great Britain by Blackie & Son Ltd., 1983
First published in the United States of America by Viking Penguin,
a division of Penguin Books USA Inc., 1992
Published in Puffin Books, 1994

1 3 5 7 9 10 8 6 4 2

THE LIBRARY OF CONGRESS HAS CATALOGED THE VIKING PENGUIN EDITION AS FOLLOWS:
Baillie, Allan.
Adrift / by Allan Baillie.—1st Amer. ed. p. cm.
Summary: While playing pirates with his little sister and
her cat in an old crate he finds on the beach, a young boy suddenly
discovers that they are adrift on the sea and that he
must somehow keep them all alive.
ISBN 0-670-84474-8
[1. Survival—Fiction. 2. Brothers and sisters—Fiction. 3. Fathers and sons—Fiction.] I. Title.
PZ7.B156Ad 1992 [Fic]—dc20 91-42345 CIP AC

Puffin Books ISBN 0-14-037010-2

Printed in the United States of America

To Lynne for Sally

A D R I F T

ONE

FLYNN stepped from a gray boulder and marched towards the sea across a seamed table of almost flat rock. He swung his plastic bucket to shoulder height with every step and glared at the fishing line, green prawns, meat scraps and the pocket knife in the bottom of the bucket. Today he might as well have left them in the kitchen, for he would not get a chance to use them. He tried to ignore his sister and the cat capering about him. This wasn't a job; it was punishment.

"Wait for me!" Sally was sliding down a cleft twenty meters behind him and she still managed to sound imperious.

"Ah, you're too slow." But he stopped.

"You got bigger legs than me." She panted up beside him. "Give me a carry."

"No." Someone might see him.

"Aw . . ." A pout. "Dad said—"

"I don't care what Dad said. He said look after you, that's all he said."

Sally shrugged. "Can I look for shells, then?"

"Do what you like." And Flynn knew he'd been conned.

Sally ran ahead before Flynn could change his mind, calling, "Come on, Nebu!" over her shoulder.

The cat leapt from a dead ball of seaweed and became a rippling black flicker over the ruler-straight trenches and the rock pools as he searched for prey. Flynn thought of calling them back, then gave up and trudged after them with an eye for fish and crabs in the pools. Just one more hour, he thought. They were moving towards a great rock slide, a mass of huge boulders brought down from the cliffs in a bite from the sea.

Flynn was on holiday. Or so they told him. More like a four week detention and he was even beginning to look forward to going back to school again. Really. This summer Mum had gone in for a very cheap holiday. So the Neil family—miserable Dad, Mum, ghastly little Sally and heroic Flynn—had just stepped across Sydney from Bankstown to Avalon and Mum's sister and her husband.

No kids you could hang around with, just a fat lady you had to call "Auntie More"—short for Maureen—and an "Uncle Norm" who had to tell everyone, even Sally, what clever TV ads he had made. All you could do was go down the beach and get dumped by a wave full of bluebottles, sit on the beach and get grilled, see some more trees or look for shells on the rocks.

And, oh yes, look after Sally.

"Like Dad'd say," Flynn muttered, hunching his

shoulders, hanging his arms, thrusting his lower lip forward and shambling about in a fair imitation of a gorilla. "Look arver Saallee, looook arver Saal, arver, arver, ick, ick . . ."

He was trying to walk with his knuckles trailing on the rocks when Sally ran back with her hands full of shells and sea-washed pebbles. She stopped and watched him in silence, looked at the cat and watched him again until he saw her feet.

Flynn stopped and straightened.

"Watcha doing?"

"What do you want?" Flynn scowled at Sally and the cat. He was sure the cat was sneering at him.

"Can I put shells in your bucket?"

"No."

"Aw . . . Why?"

"Oh, go on."

Sally emptied her hands into the bucket and skipped away to the shadows of the boulders, a wide straw hat bouncing over a fan of honey hair, brown arms, the green of faded swimming togs and the drumming of plump little legs. The cat cocked his tail at Flynn and padded after Sally with all the ease of a shadow. Flynn thought briefly of throwing a pebble at him.

The cat was the one thing Flynn and his father agreed on. They didn't like him. He was midnight black from his whiskers to the twitch of his tail, and when he moved a metallic blue rippled through his fur. He was attractive and would have been nice to have around the house, but he knew he was attractive and traded on the fact. He carried around with him all the arrogance of the Emperor of China and those yellow eyes had stared down Dad, furious with an upended plate, and a forest of dogs.

In fact, this holiday had brought a great hope to Flynn. Nebu had cowed all the dogs in Bankstown, but there was a chance that the wilder animals in the north had not heard of him. Flynn might see the Emperor treed by a dog here, perhaps by a miniature poodle.

But it had not happened yet. An eager boxer had thundered across a beach but the cat had hissed it to a stop, allowed it to circle in confusion for a minute, then chased it from the sand. So the cat had wandered with them to the rocks because dogs seemed to agree with Mum. When Mum had given the cat to Sally shortly after they had arrived in Bankstown she had called it Nebuchadnezzar because it looked like an Abyssinian mountain lion.

Which was a very dumb name for a cat. In the time it takes you to yell at the cat by name it has pinched your sausages from the kitchen table, gulped them down and got hungry again. Flynn knew that Nebuchadnezzar was a king around the time of Pharoah, but Sally couldn't pronounce it. And Abyssinia wasn't in any atlas anyway. And why have a cat? Far better to have one of those green and yellow and red parrots that sit on your shoulder.

"Arr there, matey!" said Flynn, and closed one eye and stiffened his right leg and hobbled round a rock.

Sally frantically waved him down and pointed.

The cat was almost motionless on the edge of a shaded pool. One paw was raised, the tail curled in the air, the head rising slowly and the eyes locked on something in the water. Suddenly he shuffled his hind paws and pounced into the pool.

"He has caught something! He has!" Sally scrambled up tumbled boulders for a better view.

Nebuchadnezzar stood in the pool and turned majestically towards Sally with a crab struggling in his mouth. Even Flynn was impressed.

Then the crab nipped Nebu on the nose.

Nebu immediately let the crab go and raced round in tight, yowling circles. The crab opened its claw a moment after Nebu opened his mouth to scream and was dropped onto a flat rock.

"Nebu!" Sally was alarmed.

Nebu stopped, twitched his nose and passed a paw over it to make sure the crab was no longer there. He glared at Flynn, who was quietly spluttering, and began hunting for the crab with slow murder in his eyes.

The crab did not move. Nebu crept silently towards it with his belly brushing the rock. Flynn gasped for breath and frowned.

Nebu moved up to the crab, past it a hand's breadth away, and over a nearby ridge. He was still moving his ears like gun turrets and watching for the slightest movement when the crab slid casually into the water behind him.

Flynn sat on a rock and shook with laughter. Suddenly this was the best day he'd had for months. Nebu stopped hunting and watched him in cold silence.

"Nebu, you are a silly cat," Sally said sadly and turned from the cat to the immense boulders towering over her head. White daisies exploded in bursts on the cliff and the slide and she must collect some later. She began to admire the view and turned towards the sea . . .

"Flynn!" she shouted. "Look what I found!"

T W O

It was a box. It had been caught in the entrance to a tiny bay full of yellow-green swaying seaweed and tiny black shellfish.

It was more than a box; it was wider than Flynn could stride, as high as his chest. It was built of old, stained timber locked together by fat nails, long green copper staples and angled strips of iron, red and bumpy with rust. There were some traces of letters on one side. It moved a little with the swells from the sea.

"Perhaps it's from a ship." Flynn ran his fingers over the rough wood.

"It's big." Sally could only just peer over the crate.

"It might have something in it." Flynn tried to budge the crate. It was heavy.

"What?"

"Oh, ah." Flynn knocked on the wood. "Valuable machinery."

"I don't like mackry." "Mackry" was what sat in the back of mummy's washer and it never worked.

"Or gold." Flynn scrunched up an eye and twisted his mouth. "Arr, gold, me lad, that's the thing."

"I'm not a lad."

Flynn tried to peer between the boards. "Arr, doub-loons and pieces of eight."

"Where? Let me see."

"You can't see. But it could be treasure from a shipwreck. Arr."

"I wouldn't like to be in a shipwreck."

Flynn became Flynn again. "Well, you aren't, stu-pid. The box is."

"Is what?"

"In a shipwreck."

"Why?"

Flynn banged his head against the crate several times. It felt better.

"What does the letters say?"

"Oh, the writing? Nothing. Something, some-thing, C, A, N, something, something, something, P, S. This is a crate full of cans of peas."

Sally wrinkled her nose.

Flynn started to paddle round the crate and found that the side facing the sea simply wasn't there.

Inside the crate there was a smooth floor of washed sand and seaweed shifting with the water. That was all. He crawled into the crate and dug the sand out like a dog in the hope of finding something, but in the end there was nothing but four mysterious depres-sions in the wood, made by studs or legs or the corners of a heavy object. He was about to back out of the crate when it skidded a little along the sand and he lurched against the side.

"It's moving," he said in surprise.

Sally looked inside with all the careful judgement of a real estate agent. "Maybe we could make a cubby house."

Flynn looked at his little sister wearily. Would she always take him for just a bigger playmate? "What, here?"

"Take it home. To Auntie More's house."

"How're you going to get it there, fly?"

"That's silly. Daddy might carry it."

"Dad? Dad never does anything. Forget it."

Sally turned and walked away, as if Flynn had hurt her.

What the hell.

Flynn banged his open hand against the crate and it rocked.

Why does the villain always have to be me, he thought. Never Dad. You do everything, polish the car, mow the lawn, get the bread, do the dishes— everything—and he just sits there with his books and his figures. Oh, we must never disturb Father. Mum goes about saying "Shhh, shhh!" to the walls and you have to take your baby sister out and play . . . It's floating.

The only time he notices you is when you've gone

and done something wrong. Just looks up from his crummy books and yells and looks in his books again. Never laughs now. Now? Did he ever laugh? Did he ever think you'd done anything right? . . .

Hey, hey, this great crate is floating. Wake up.

Flynn leaned against the crate and watched it drift over the sand. He pushed it to deeper water, stepped back and leapt for the top, skinning his right knee. The crate creaked and grounded on the sand. Flynn held his shin and bit his knee until the pain subsided.

It wouldn't be that bad if Dad did something. I mean you could put up with a grouch who flew jumbos or chased killers, or climbed mountains. Even looked after sheep like Dad used to do, you don't ask for much. But he does nothing now, makes up bills in a little green office, that's worse than being a teacher.

Flynn rocked the crate, but it didn't move. He looked at Sally, sitting on a rock, stroking and mouthing words to the cat, and shrugged.

He comes home and reads his books and adds up his bills and talks all the time about high interest and strikes and mortgages. He doesn't want to go anywhere, just drink his beer and weed his garden and worry.

Flynn sat up on the crate and frowned as a sad little thought drifted towards him.

In Bankstown the kids called Dad "Mister Neil."
In the country they had called him "Sean."

Flynn shrugged and tried to rock the crate. It moved
a little.

What about a crab in Walker's desk? That'd get him.
No, he'd run screaming to the teacher. And you'd
have to keep it until school started. Now this crate,
you could do something with it . . .

Flynn rubbed his nose and looked at Sally. He
smiled slowly.

It's not a crate, it's a ship. Maybe a galleon . . .

"Avast!"

Sally ignored him. Nebu had rolled over and was
pawing her arm.

"Avast! Strike your colors!"

Nebu arched his back, closed his eyes and purred,
feeling the warmth of the sun on the rock and Sally's
gentle fingers on his belly. Sally only glanced at Flynn.
She was used to his games.

"Arr, mateys, so she wants to fight! Smedley, pre-
pare for a broadside of chain shot! Oye Oye sur. Well,
get about it!" Flynn looked in the bucket and found
a small round pebble. "All loaded, sur, cap'n. Fire,
Smedley!"

The pebbled splashed at Sally's feet and Nebu
jumped to his feet.

"Stop that!"

"You missed, Smedley. You'll be flogged. More powder, man! Fire!"

A corkscrew shell shattered on a rock near Sally's leg as she jumped to her feet.

"That's my shells! Leave them alone!"

"Arr there, do you surrender?" Flynn lobbed a shell near Nebu, who hissed and sprang away.

"Stop it!" Sally's bottom lip quivered.

Flynn hesitated. "Surrender or you die."

"Which?"

Flynn sighed. Why is it that you have to explain everything? "See? I'm floating—almost. I'm Black-beard the Pirate and this is my galleon."

"You haven't even got a beard."

"Doesn't matter. It's me name. I'm the most murderous pirate on the Spanish Main. I make people walk the plank, keelhaul them, castaway them on desert islands and drink their blood!"

"Yech!" Sally screwed up her nose. "Can I get on?"

"No." Flynn tried to make the crate move by violently twisting his body.

"Why?"

"You'd probably fall off. Anyway, you'd sink my galleon."

"It's not a galleon. It's a dirty old box, and if you don't let me on I'm going to tell Daddy."

All the time. Dad thinks she's some sort of jewel. Big deal! Flynn rocked the crate sideways and it slid a little.

Sally tried the quivering lip trick again.

"Oh, all right."

Sally immediately beamed and splashed towards the crate.

"First things first. You have to push the galleon into deeper waters so it'll float with you on board."

Sally looked at the crate. "You have to help."

"Oh, go on. You're a big girl now."

Sally pushed very hard at the crate, until wood marks were left on her palms and her bathing suit was getting wet. She frowned as if she felt she was being unfairly used.

"Okay. You can come aboard now."

Sally reached up for Flynn's hands, then dropped her arms. "I forgot Nebu."

"We've no room for a cat. Leave it on the rocks."

"No." Sally turned from the crate and called, "Nebu . . . ?"

Nebu was lying on his back, juggling a small shell with his four paws. He protested loudly and squirmed when Sally bundled him up and carried him to the crate, his tail trailing in the water.

Flynn folded his arms across his chest like some sultan and turned away from Sally.

"Aw, come on, Flynny." Sally offered Nebu as if he was a rich and mysterious gift.

"The name is Blackbeard, and no."

Sally folded her arms about Nebu, who was beginning to struggle seriously. "But Nebu is a ship's cat." And she smiled.

Flynn blinked and looked at Sally oddly. "What?"

"He is a ship's cat. Every ship has got to have a ship's cat, or the big rats will eat it up one night . . ."

"All right, all right, give me the cat."

Sally handed Nebu up to Flynn but the cat twisted from their combined grip to land on the edge of the crate. Nebu was about to leap for freedom when he realized he was surrounded by water. He mewed and quivered as Sally was hauled onto the crate, but he stayed put.

"Arr there, matey, now we're sailing for the Caribbean." Flynn watched the waving crown of an anemone pass under the crate and thought about skeletons guarding chests of gold, ancient treasure maps, and creeping up to an anchored galleon under muffled oars. He felt every bit a pirate under his crimson shirt and black swim shorts. Of course, Sally was pretty poor material for the crew, a gruesome crew son, but you had to make do with whatever came along these days.

Sally started waving and rocking the crate.

"What're you waving at, Sol?"

"My shadow. Who's Sol?"

The crate slowly turned them to face the sea. Their shadows were flowing over ridges, rocks and the open water and Sally could see the shadow of her arm moving on a sea-washed rock.

"You are."

"I'm Sally."

"Whoever heard of a little girl on a pirate ship? You're Sol, my cabin boy."

"I'm a lady."

"On a pirate ship ladies get to walk the plank."

"I'm a lady pirate. What do pirates do?"

The crate had turned again and they were nudging past a barnacle-encrusted finger of black rock to face a quiet golden sea and two seagulls drifting across the empty sky. Flynn lay back and watched a sinking sun, a copper gong, almost touching the cliffs. He stretched and felt the warmth of the sun on his face, and thought: Look at that. You could be anywhere, anytime. Lugs like Walker, the Post Who Walks, and miserable Dad and Algebra and motor mowers that won't start, they haven't been invented yet, and probably never will.

"Pirates go anywhere." Flynn spoke with his eyes closed and didn't really care if Sally was listening. "If they want to see Madagascar in March, well, they just do. If they want to sit in a tree with a huge bottle of orange and twenty packets of potato chips, well, that's what they do. Nobody ever says to them 'you can't do this' and 'you can't even think of doing that.' They do everything they want to do whenever they want to . . ."

Sally sounded doubtful. "Maybe we should go home."

"Nobody tells a pirate when to go home."

"Mum'll be worried."

Flynn sighed and opened an eye. "She won't even expect us yet."

A long, slow swell tilted the crate and Nebu growled, a crouching stone panther against the sun. Perhaps a figurehead.

"Anyway, it's a silly name." Sally picked at a plank.

"What?"

"Blackbeard."

Flynn closed the eye again and began to smile.

"You don't even have a beard, anyway. And I don't like beards. They tickle like Uncle Norm's . . ."

"Wonder where it's been."

"Which?"

"This." Flynn slapped the crate. "It could've been in a shipwreck a thousand years ago. It could've been down to the Antarctic and seen the seals and seen an ice mountain slide into the sea, or seen cannibals in the South Pacific, or seen Krakatoa explode, or a sea battle, or San Francisco, or even a Kraken. . . . The stories it could tell!"

"Flynn . . ." Sally's voice was soft and serious. She was looking over her shoulder.

She said: "We're going away."

FLYNN smiled and frowned and tried to work out what his silly little sister was trying to say. He leaned back and turned from the open sea.

"Oh," he said. He was a little surprised.

The crate was no longer bobbing about in a sheltered backwater by the rocks, but was now about fifteen meters away.

"Arr, matey, perhaps us pirates'd better set course for 'ome, eh?" he said and slipped easily off the crate.

He splashed lightly and his feet searched for a bottom that was not there. Past the tiny bubbles streaming from his toes there was something misty and white, washed with deepening blue.

Flynn broke surface, gasping in surprise. "Can't reach the sand. Wasn't ready for that."

He saw the sudden fear in Sally's eyes and thought: She's going to blubber all over the place. Why do I have to carry her all the time? He said, "S'all right. I'll just have to push the crate back to the rocks. No worries."

Nebu watched the rocks with his claws sunk into the wood and made a desperate sound in his throat, but Sally stroked the cat, said, "Stop it Nebu," and managed to smile back at Flynn.

Flynn swam around to the shady side of the crate, placed his hands wide apart on the boards and began to kick, powerfully and deep so his feet never touched the surface. A series of gentle swells passed under Flynn and the crate and rolled on smoothly to the rocks. Sally smoothed the panic from the cat, but his claws remained embedded in the wood.

After ten minutes Flynn panted, "How're we doing?"

Sally had not taken her eyes from the rocks from the moment Flynn had started pushing. "I don't know." She sounded troubled.

Flynn put his head in the water and blew a stream of angry bubbles. His arms were beginning to ache. "What do you mean, don't know? How far have we got to go?"

"A long way."

"Still?" Flynn stopped pushing and ducked his head to the side of the crate. He felt as if something heavy and hard had hit him in the stomach and he turned away.

The crate was now twenty-five meters from the rocks, as if Flynn had spent all that time pushing it out to sea.

Flynn tried to push the crate with his shoulder,

kicking very hard, very fast, as he locked his eyes on a black boulder and willed it to come closer. But Flynn was pushing at a corner of the crate instead of a side, so it rocked and turned like a wheel, with him beside it, not behind it. He tried to pull the crate, but he could only hold it at a corner with his fingertips and when he kicked he banged his toes against the bottom. And all the time the crate was drifting from the shore.

Flynn swam around behind the crate and resumed kicking while he thought of what he could do.

"I want to go home," Sally said, very softly.

"What do you think I'm trying to do?" Flynn shouted and immediately regretted it. "You'll have to come down into the water."

"It's too deep."

"You grab me round the neck. I'll take you ashore."

"I'm scared."

"You'll be all right. Come on." Flynn was panting. His legs were becoming heavy.

Sally looked at the rocks. They were so far away. She pressed her lips together and lowered her legs over the side of the crate as Flynn reached for her ankle.

Nebu suddenly screamed in terror. The cat arched his back and clawed at the wood, staring at Sally as she prepared to abandon him to drift alone on the ocean. Sally stopped wriggling from the crate and Nebu's cry became a pathetic silent mew.

"Come on. We haven't much time." Flynn pulled at Sally's leg.

"What about Nebu?"

"Come *on!*" Flynn pulled hard on the leg, but Sally kicked herself free and rolled to the center of the crate.

"I'm not coming without Nebu."

Flynn looked back at the rocks, now not much more than silhouettes in the sea. The crate was in some sort of rip. "We're not playing games anymore, come on down." He breathed slowly to steady himself. "Cats can swim."

"They can't too." Sally's voice was breaking.

"You saw the tiger on TV. You come on down now and Nebu'll jump in after you. Come on."

"Well . . ."

"What d'you want?" Flynn was shouting. He rocked the crate violently. The cat hissed and Sally began to sob.

"It's hopeless," Flynn muttered, then louder, "hopeless! You're going to drown here, you know that?"

Sally was quiet for a moment. "All right," she said softly. She turned to Nebu and tore the cat from the wood and leapt into the water, a bundle of twisting, clawing, shrieking animal and suddenly bleeding little girl. When Sally surfaced she was coughing and crying in pain and without the cat, and her hat.

Flynn pulled her towards him. "Quick, around my neck."

"Where's Nebu?" She was finding it hard to talk, as if she had swallowed some water.

"I don't know. He's all right. Hang on."

Flynn was struggling to keep his head above water with Sally bearing down on his neck. He looked at the now distant shore and wondered vaguely if he was strong enough to swim the distance against the current like this. Then Sally shouted and pushed Flynn below the water as she fought something wild.

Flynn turned and saw something angular and black moving on Sally's shoulder. There was blood in the water. He kicked until he could breathe and tried to lift the cat off Sally, but the cat was sinking its claws into her head. Sally had closed her eyes and was whimpering from the pain. She screamed when Flynn tried to pry a claw from her head. The cat made a sound he had never heard before, like a snake about to strike, and then bit his hand. Sally screamed until water flooded into her mouth.

Flynn looked desperately at the shore, now fading as the last streaks of sunlight lifted from the cliff, and turned tiredly for the crate.

He reached the crate in the longest half minute he had ever endured. Then Nebu leaped from Sally's head and she stopped coughing and yelling. Sally shakily climbed from Flynn's shoulders to join Nebu on the crate. Flynn rested in the water for a while, breathing heavily and listening to the subdued sobbing from the top of the crate.

Eventually he had to board the crate. He placed a foot at the bottom of the empty side, flattened his hands on the vertical sides and surged upward. The crate tilted and danced with him in the water, with Sally bawling and the cat screeching at him. He finally lay sprawled on the crate, splinters in his palms, scratches down his chest and a throbbing pain in the side of his right foot, where he'd kicked something.

But he couldn't rest. The last rim of the sun was sliding behind a hill but there was still light in the sky. Flynn slowly got to his feet on the crate and waved his arms and shouted for help from a shore he saw only as a thin black line in a sea of burgundy.

After a while he could not even see that. He sat down.

FLYNN drew up his knees and hugged them. He rested his head on them, shivered and stared at the cat, not a panther now, just a sodden skeleton of frightened animal staring at him with huge eyes. As if it thought he was about to kill it. Which he might. Flynn shifted his gaze to Sally and Sally had lost her hat and he couldn't remember when it was lost. She was looking at the lights marching up a hill he couldn't see and she was crying, shaking her shoulders with the sobbing.

Flynn was thinking: Oh, but you are in trouble now, big trouble. Oh boy.

Now, just now, Dad would be shouting at Mum for trusting Flynn out of the house with Sally and Uncle Norm would be reminding him it was his idea and Mum would say, "Never mind, let's find them." And Dad would roar, "Fine, but when I catch that boy . . ."

Just like the last time.

Flynn closed his eyes and for a while he wasn't sitting on a crate, drifting into the Pacific.

Dad was shouting at Mum, slapping his spectacles repeatedly on a handful of papers, and Mum was waving her hand at Flynn and shouting back, but there was no sound at all. Like one of the old films that flickered and jerked with the piano hammering away in the background. But Flynn somehow knew what they were saying and even what was going to happen. He knew Dad was going to throw his papers in the air and say something about him.

And Dad drew his spectacles back from the papers and flipped them over his shoulder, a brief blizzard of white sheets, and now you could hear the sounds.

"Can't you control your boy?" Dad shouted.

Oh yes, Flynn remembered. The skateboard incident.

"Sean, he's your boy too."

"Not when he does something like this, he's not." Waving at the papers on the floor.

He'd only been skating down the hill, chasing Barry. *That* Barry? That must have been a long time ago. Barry Walker, The Post Who Walks. He'd been chasing Walker and they'd been friends but Barry had made a tight little turn on the footpath and he'd hit a rock and shot onto the road. But they'd still been friends until later.

"Well, Sean . . ."

"Well nothing. What do you say when a constable marches your son up to the front door? You feel like a damn criminal."

"You've already had it out with him."

"I should take it out of his hide. There's Mr. Vespucci's Escort . . ." The Escort had squealed to a stop no more than a meter from Flynn's hurtling skateboard.

". . . and old Joe Haynes' vintage Holden. You know he still blackwalls the tires . . ."

The Holden had banged into the back of the Escort, buckling the hood. The car looked like an angry beetle.

"And the damned truck. He's not a boy, he's a disaster."

The truck had rammed the back of the Holden, breaking the lights, bending the bumper and denting the trunk.

"And to finish the whole horrible mess, there was Mrs. Hammett." Dad leaned back weakly and shook his head as if he couldn't really believe what he had said.

Mrs. Hammett had been walking along the far footpath, carrying two great paper bags of groceries, when she heard the squealing and the crumple of metal and saw Flynn scudding towards her, looking back at what he'd caused. She had screamed, thrown her bags into the air and run for safety.

"All right, it's over now," Mum, that beautiful, calm person, said. "Give it a rest."

"Over? It's over till that idiot boy does something tomorrow."

Mum smiled. "We've seen worse, haven't we, Sean?"

Dad frowned at her, then, very slowly, began to smile. "I guess we have." Flynn caught a fading glimpse of a father he had forgotten about, and nodded. And it was sort of funny, wasn't it?

"I just wish he'd grown up a little."

And Flynn was rocking on a lonely crate and this time it wasn't funny at all.

He was sitting hunched, as if he was sick, with one hand resting on the rim of the bucket. The moon was leading a few timid stars into the dark blue sky over a quiet, deep sea that stretched out, and out, and out . . .

Sally had become too tired to cry anymore, so she stopped. "Where's Nebu?"

Flynn looked at her in astonishment. He had actually forgotten that she was there and it made a bad situation far worse. "I should have thrown him overboard."

"You didn't!" A moment of anger.

"No. There." Flynn pointed at the dark patch behind the bucket and two small yellow globes switched on. "Did he hurt you much?" He could deal with Sally now that she wasn't blubbering.

Sally looked at the cat's motionless eyes and shook her head. "He didn't mean it. He was frightened, weren't you, Nebu?" Sally reached across the crate, found an ear and tickled it.

"Rotten cat." Flynn looked at the scratches on his arms.

"He's not. He's a very nice cat, aren't you, Nebu?" Sally picked up the cat carefully and it became tense. But it began to relax on her crossed legs and licked salt from its fur. "He doesn't like water. See, cats can't swim."

"We would be at home now, if it wasn't for that cat." Flynn weighed the responsibility for tonight's disaster. It was his fault that they'd got on the crate in the first place, he admitted, but it was Sally who had found the crate in the first place. And she had insisted on getting on when the crate was afloat. But she was only a little girl and she was the one who had noticed they were floating away. Too late. No, the cat should have warned them, a dog would have, and then the cat stopped them swimming ashore. No, it was definitely the cat's fault.

"Nebu only wanted to live," Sally said. "That's all."

Flynn glared at the cat and finally shook his head. You can't blame a cat, really, can you? And what's the point? You're here, and that's it. That's all of it.

"Well, let's have a look at what he did to you."

Sally bowed her head towards Flynn and he carefully parted her tangled hair. There were three deep scratches in her scalp and the hair around them had become a solid mass, but the bleeding had stopped. Flynn slowly emptied the bucket into Sally's lap, washed it out and rinsed her hair with seawater. It was something to do.

"Flynn? . . ." Sally was grave, even while she fed a very cautious Nebu with a green prawn.

"Um."

"What happens to us now?"

Flynn lifted his fingers from her hair and thought for a while. He could see small lights rimming the tall back cliffs of North Avalon. He could hear the low swell working among the great boulders at the foot of the cliffs. He could see the headlights and the glowing red tails of cars moving fast on Barrenjoey Road, so close to the beach they looked as if they were flying over the sand. So close you still felt like waving and shouting, but far, far, too far away.

"Ah, Dad'll find us, no worry." Tell her anything. She still believes in goblins.

Sally shook her head. "Dad doesn't know where we are."

Flynn frowned. She was right of course, and that was a little bit of trouble. Sally was annoying when she was stupid and Flynn wanted her to be smart, but she was far worse when she was smart and he wanted her to be stupid.

Now Dad and Uncle Norm were driving about in Norm's polished Volvo with Mum hanging over the phone and Auntie More twittering behind a teapot. They'd perhaps come to the beach and hoot their horn and yell. Then they'd go to the moviehouse because they'd reckon Flynn would try to get in without paying. They'd stop by the school and look at the playground, there'd always be a couple of kids swinging about, and they'd catch the kids on skateboards at the car parks. They'd cruise past the ice-cream shops, maybe go as far as Newport. Then they'd check out the hospital, never mind what Mum would do on the phone, and go to the cops.

Flynn tried again. "It doesn't matter. When we don't come back Dad'll tell the police. And they've got helicopters and search-and-rescue squads and everything. They'll find us in a couple of hours. It's very calm out here. We're in no trouble."

Sally tilted her head. "But how—"

"You cold?"

"No. A little bit."

"You'll dry out. We all will. This box is so big it will keep us warm and dry and they won't be able to miss us."

Sally looked at the crate, frowned and stretched her arms until they almost touched the sides. "It's not very big."

Flynn sighed. "Look at the stars now." Anything to get her mind off things. Flynn waved at a broad wash of sparklers over his head, thickening in the sky almost as he stared. Like a sudden brushfire.

"You see the stars over there, the lopsided cross? That's the Southern Cross, and with the Pointers over there you can find out exactly where south is."

"Why?"

"Arr, lad, so we can find Cap'n Flint's treasure. It's out there, buried beneath two crossed palms on a little desert island in the middle of the Caribbean. Doubloons, pieces of eight, diamonds, rubies, pearls from the South Seas, necklaces of emeralds, goblets of gold . . . all guarded by a skeleton with a cutlass!"

"I want to go home," Sally said.

"Avast, lad, you will. But first we'll plunder Panama!"

"I don't want to play games anymore."

"Games! We don't play games on my ship, we keelhaul . . ." And Flynn found himself outside his head and listening to himself. He didn't sound like a pirate at all, just a little boy trying to hide under a warm blanket of make-believe. "All right, what do you want to do?"

"I don't know. You're supposed to know."

No. It wasn't fair, making him boss of all this. "Just wait. That's all."

"All right. I will wait." Sally lay back on the crate and stared at the stars. "What's that?"

A strong light stood high above the house lights and far away. Then it went out.

Flynn stirred on the crate and waited for the light. After a few seconds it beamed on again. Too high for a house, too strong for a star, too small and bright for the moon, and was it moving?

"They're looking for us!" he shouted.

Sally blinked and the light went out.

"Don't worry. It's a helicopter with a searchlight. It will come down to us. Find us in half an hour, pull us up on a rope and take us home . . ."

Flynn thought briefly that he'd rather be found with a broken arm. That way he could not get quite the frying he was going to get from Dad. A broken arm, or concussion, or amnesia . . .

The light came on, held a second or so and went off, went on and went off again. It blinked a few times then remained off for a long time. It wasn't moving.

"It's not a helicopt," Sally said and lay back on the crate.

"No," Flynn said. Well, he wasn't going to get fried yet. "Barrenjoey lighthouse." He wondered how the prawns would taste.

He sighed and sprawled on the crate, facing away

from the light, and tried to ignore his disappointment. He watched Nebu squirming happily into Sally's armpit, stretching his paws on her shirt and rumbling, a drowsy volcano.

"Stop that," Sally said, lightly cuffing Nebu's paws. Nebu ignored her.

Flynn straightened his legs until his feet hung over the end of the crate. The wood was hard on the back of his head and he was a little cold, but the easy movement of the crate in the water made it almost comfortable.

"There's an awful lot of them now," Sally said quietly.

"What?"

"Stars."

"Oh, yes." They were now an eruption across a sky so bright the moon threw a shadow. "Count them."

"I can't count that high. Next year."

"Can you see the pictures? Let's forget about lighthouses and angry parents."

"No. What pictures?"

"Like your dot drawings. Look, there's a man with a sword, Orion, and there's his belt, the three stars. And there's a scorpion and a fish. And way over there, there's Canopus, and—"

"They don't look like that at all. Anyway how did

this box come all the way from that star?"

"Who said?"

"You said. You said it said on the box that it came from Can of Peas."

"Oh. Well, that's different."

"Mmmmnnnphnn . . ."

"What are you doing?"

"This is a spaceship, not a gallony. I'm going to the moon."

"Fine."

The stars dipped and steadied, dipped and steadied as the heavy crate sluiced the sea. Flynn turned his head to see the lighthouse and the lights on the hills, but they seemed a little further away now. He turned away and resolved not to look back again.

"Where's the star Superman came from?"

"Oh. There."

"But Superman's planet went bang."

"Oh, yes. I meant that was about where it was."

"Poor Superman."

They won't find us, Flynn thought bleakly. The police are going to look for us where Dad will have looked, in the streets. They will look for us in the little bush parks, the beaches, along the cliffs. Maybe they will check on the boats in Pittwater, but no boat will be missing and there's nothing to get them to look out to sea. Not for two kids on a crate . . .

"Flynn?" Sally's voice was heavy and tired. Perhaps she was talking in her sleep.

"Yes."

"What will it be like?" No more than a whisper.

"What?" Flynn was trying to smile.

"Drowning."

DROWNING.

The thing was, he *did* know what it was like. He'd just forgotten. It was so long ago . . .

Before the crowds of Bankstown and the school bus and algebra and The Post Who Walks there had been a tree. A very old Red Gum that tilted high over Guinnigan's Hole with a hollow at its base and a long rope dangling over the water. In summer the kids would pedal in from all over the place and swing over the waterhole on the rope, and drop at their highest and furthest. They'd swim about until they were tired and then they'd sit under the giant gum and eat sandwiches, and fish for yabbies and swap tales. They had decided long ago that Guinnigan was a bushranger who rode with Ben Hall, and he'd been shot by nine troopers, but he'd hidden his gold under the gum before he'd jumped into the waterhole. Nearly everyone claimed that they had seen Guinnigan's ghost.

But one afternoon Flynn had got bored with the waterhole and decided to climb the tree. Just to see what it was like up there. In the beginning the climbing was easy, the trunk sloped towards the waterhole and Dad had cut steps with his axe to reach the big branch with the rope round it. Beyond? Well, he'd never gone beyond the branch before now.

He climbed quickly towards the branch, at first almost walking up the slope, then spreading his hands wide on the rough bark. Someone yelled out behind him and a girl giggled.

He stepped onto the branch, panting slightly. His feet worked for balance on the smooth, worn bark. Below the rope, far below the rope, the lazy sun dappled the water; bright circles flowed into each other as children jumped from the bank, or surfaced like seals, or just floated. An old friend clapped his hands and called on him to jump.

He waved and laughed and shook his head. He lifted his eyes from the noisy warmth of the waterhole and began to climb again. The bark was rough now, and the branches were further apart the higher he went. A twig snapped off in his hand and he swung in a wild half-circle before he could catch anything. He was bleeding a little on the back of his left hand. He stopped in a fork and thought about going back. A girl was shouting that he'd better come down, it was dangerous, and he couldn't see anything but leaves from where he was. But he climbed on.

After a while he could feel the trunk move in the breeze. He pushed up through a long forest of rattling twigs and a shimmering sea of leaves and felt a bit like Jack on his Beanstalk.

It was a new country.

Forget about Jack. Flynn was the giant. He could reach up and pocket a cloud, or stride out on that little dirt track towards Forbes, get to school in three steps and squash it flat. If he wanted to. And there was home, the red corrugated iron roof, the dusty verandah—Mum spent all her time sweeping it down—and Mum, big Mum because there was going to be a little brother or sister, was pulling a bucket of water from the well. It was a magic well, that one. No matter how hot it was, that water was icy cold.

And further out in the big flat paddock was Dad on his tractor, hauling the blades of the disk plough across the yellow grass, leaving low walls of brown soil bare and steaming. A small group of sheep peered through the fence at the tractor, bleated at it and shambled hastily up a safe hill. If Flynn closed one eye and lowered his head and did not move at all he could almost say that everything he saw was his.

"My good man," he said, pointing an imperious finger at the tiny figure on the tractor, "make sure that you plough straight lines. Or off with your head!"

He giggled as the top of the gum swayed in a gust of wind. He opened his mouth to catch a fist of air and he was almost flying. He could go down faster than he'd come up, just by diving at the leafy branch waving at the sun below. He realized he was looking at the branch seriously and he began to be afraid.

So he quickly beat his chest, gave the cry of the bull ape and hurled himself at the branch before the fright stopped him.

Flynn felt an instant of pure fear, the rush of air, then the leaves brushed his face and he swung his arms to hug the branch. He'd made it . . .

And the branch was gone, whipped away from his arms as if it had never existed. Someone was screaming in his ear and he was spiralling through the leaves and twigs and the girl was looking up at him with her mouth open and her eyes wide in horror, and the water flashed at him. And it hit him so hard his face, his chest, his arms, legs were shocked numb.

For a while he was drifting down, motionless, through deepening brown water to black. He knew he should move his body, push it into the light where he could breathe but he could not remember how to move anything anymore and his chest hurt . . .

He was coughing and being sick and his arms, legs and face stung as if half of him had been fried in a huge pan. He was lying on the muddy bank of the waterhole and he was surrounded by thousands of kids. Even his hair hurt.

"All right. Don't move." Dad was squatting beside his shoulder. "Move your right big toe. Hurt?"

"No." He sounded hoarse and he coughed again.

"Left. Right leg. Left. Right hand. Left. Arm. Left. Head. How's the ribs? You're very lucky. Thanks, Dot."

The girl shrugged, smiled, said, "s'all right, Sean," and dived back into the water. She was followed by most of the others.

Dad nodded after the girl. "Dot found you. Pulled you out by the hair."

"Oh." Flynn rubbed his head. He sat up with a great deal of effort. "I'm going to get it, aren't I?"

Dad turned slowly and looked at Flynn as if making up his mind. "Oh, I think you've had enough, don't you?"

Flynn nodded.

" 'Course you'll have to tell Mum before the other kids do. And maybe you ought to buy Dot a box of chocolates."

"Euch."

"Yeah, that's a real tough one."

"Ah, not so tough."

"How high did you get?"

"Up to the top." Flynn pointed. He was surprised; it was higher than he had thought.

"All that way!" Dad put his hand on Flynn's shoulder. "When I was your age I jumped from a pier, but it wasn't nearly as high as Old Red."

"I didn't jump. I fell."

"Okay, it was a silly stunt. But you've been up there. You've done it. Just don't do it again, son."

Dad patted Flynn on the shoulder and Flynn stared up at the giant tree he had conquered. No, he wouldn't ever try climbing this tree again. What was the point? But perhaps there would be a bigger tree someday.

Dad's patting became lighter, vaguer and the waterhole darkened as the air became cool. The mud bank hardened and began to rock. Flynn struggled desperately to pull himself back into Dad's arms, but he was left with only the rocking and the damp cold. He opened his eyes and saw nothing but blackness and a single staring eye.

IN a flash of horror, Flynn thought: It's Sally, she died in the cold . . .

Sally sniffled. "I can't stop shivering."

Flynn rolled towards her, covering part of her body with his own as Nebu growled sleepily in protest. He found the cat curled on Sally's stomach, scratched its ear and held his chattering teeth apart long enough to say: "It'll get better."

He wanted to go back to that shady waterhole but he was too much awake now. Dad had betrayed him and left, but he was getting used to it now. Give you a last chance, Big Daddy, he thought. You just tell us what *you'd* do. Eh?

"The stars are all gone," Sally said.

Flynn looked up and saw absolutely nothing, as if the sky had been wiped clean or he was wearing a blindfold.

"What does that mean?"

"Maybe clouds," Flynn said, realizing that if it was clouds—and he could think of nothing else—the clouds must cover the sky from horizon to horizon. That meant a lot of rain and probably a storm. He began waiting for the first flash of lightning.

Tell you what you'd do, Dad, he thought, and stopped.

That was just it. He didn't know what the dad by the waterhole would do. That was the man that laughed a lot. The one the kids would call Sean, who'd chase them through the long grass with bloodcurdling yells, and who had climbed mountains, jumped from piers and found gold in a creek near Parkes. He could play rugby, basketball, baseball, cricket, even soccer and he knew just about everything about just about everything. No, Flynn didn't know what *that* dad'd do out here. He wouldn't get caught like this anyway, but then he'd know something Flynn didn't know and just fix everything.

But Flynn knew what *this* dad, the man that shouted a lot and did huge sums, would do. He would just sit here, like this, and wait. It's like having two dads. Same face, just a couple of new lines, same hair, less hair but the same, same scar across the back from the time a goose chased him through a barbed wire fence. But now everything's changed.

"I'm awful cold. Where are we going, Arcita?"

"No, we're not going to Antarctica. You frightened?"

The dad *now* would be frightened, wouldn't you, Dad?

"I'm not frightened. I'm not. I'm just awful cold. Will the sun come?"

"Yes, don't worry. Soon." But how much of the night had gone?

Flynn had been almost certain he had not fallen asleep in the night. In the beginning he had lain on the crate and listened to Sally snore quietly and watched the moon, then he had listened for any sound on the water, such as a motor. Then there were long hours of silence and growing cold, when he closed his eyes but was aware of any change in the motion of the air or the ocean. Then he was at the waterhole, so he must've dropped off. Perhaps he could estimate the time he'd spent awake, but how much time do you spend in a dream? It could be midnight, or just before dawn.

Not like your bills or mortgage payments, is it Dad? Dad?

The morning took a long time coming, but it arrived. The black became gray, then a dirty white and Flynn blinked at Sally as if she were out of focus, or behind streaked glass. He could not see the water.

"Where's the water?" Sally said. It wasn't getting any warmer, just a little brighter.

"It's a sea mist," Flynn said quietly.

The crate was bobbing very slowly in a sea of vapor, thick enough for Flynn's hand to disappear if he straightened his arm. The vapor formed an impenetrable bubble about the crate and Flynn could see heavy streamers of fog drifting between him and Sally. They were utterly lost. They did not know where the shore was, or the sea, or the sky. The white mists were more frightening than the darkness that had gone before.

"Where are we?" Sally asked, and her voice was beginning to quiver.

"Don't—" Flynn stopped. His voice was unnaturally high-pitched as if he were about to cry.

We can't do that, can we, Dad?

Flynn tried again, speaking with deliberate slowness. "Don't worry. It'll lift. It's common at sea. It'll go away, and you'll see we're very close to the beach. You'll see."

Sally started to nod as if agreeing with Flynn, but she kept on nodding, faster and faster.

Flynn blinked and gripped her shoulders until she stopped. "Hey!"

"I want to go home," she sniffled, and her eyes were suddenly awash.

"Stop that!" Flynn was angry. "What's the good of that? Dad's not here, is he?"

Sally rubbed her eyes. "I can't help it."

"What do you expect me to do?"

Sally looked at him with her cheeks running and turned away.

Flynn closed his eyes and pulled her to his side.

Sometimes, he told himself, you've just got to dry up.

"You're a silly boy," Sally said, but sniffled freely in his shirt.

Flynn nodded. "Yeah, I know. I'm sorry." It was a great effort, but he surprised himself. He'd actually meant it. "We'll get home. Just wait until the mist lifts. What about a song?"

Sally stopped sniffling. "What?"

"A song. What about the song about the pigs?"

Sally wiped her eyes and looked at him suspiciously. "You don't like my songs. Only Mummy likes my songs."

"That's different. There's no time at home. Now we've got all the time we want. I like your songs. I'll help you sing."

"All right." She grabbed his index finger and sang, in a lonely little voice, "This little piggy went to market, this little piggy—"

Flynn joined in, slapping his free hand on his leg, so Nebu awoke and growled—"piggy had roast beef—"

Sally stopped singing and glared at Flynn. "That is the three little piggy."

"Oh. Sorry." You never know with a mist like this, Flynn thought. There could be fishermen just out there, just a few meters away. They'll fish anywhere, anytime, you never know.

"All right then. This little piggy went to market, this little piggy stayed home . . ."

Flynn sang along very loudly and peered round him.

After a while they were no longer troubled by the cold and Flynn saw the pale globe of the rising sun through the mist. When they had run out of songs and the strength to sing them the sea had become a steaming plate, spreading as the mist thinned in the heat.

"Now we're getting somewhere, kid," Flynn said. "Watch for the shore. Home for lunch."

"I'm hungry."

"So'm I."

The mist lifted slowly and the plate became a plain of water, catching the gold shimmering from the warm yellow sun.

"We're a bit out. Don't worry. There'll be boats out and they'll see us." Flynn smiled, with about the same sincerity as the wolf at the door.

A little later he said, "It won't be long now, just think what you'll be able to tell your friends." But he wasn't smiling anymore.

Flynn did not say a word when the mist had lifted entirely, burned to a white puff-ball by an angry sun. The crate was sitting in the center of a featureless polished ocean. The horizon was a distant unbroken ring, a faint line separating blue water from a blue sky.

SEVEN

THEY sat on the crate for several hours, staring at the vast horizon for any sign of a boat or a distant hill until their eyes hurt. The sun lifted to burn the blue of the sky and turn the motionless water to a great silver disk, but there was nothing else to see. Flynn felt a terrible loneliness, as if he and Sally were the only people left on Earth.

He noticed Sally's eyes were overflowing and bit his lip.

"Sally?"

What would you do, Dad? Forget about your crummy books for a sec.

"Yes?" Sally wouldn't look at him.

"Just look at the water. Have you ever seen it so smooth?"

"No."

"You could almost walk on it."

"You would sink."

"Yes, yes. But it's so still it *looks* like you could walk back to the beach. How long do you think it would take to walk home?"

"That's silly."

"It's not as far away as it looks. There are cliffs

over there, but you can't see them because of the haze."

"What's a haze?"

"Well, it's water which evaporates—"

"Where's the beach?"

"Over there." Flynn pointed very definitely at a point on the horizon because he thought the sun was moving that way. It would set where it had set the night before. He wanted to be positive about something.

Sally nodded doubtfully, but she wiped her eyes, and waited.

Nebu nosed around the bucket for possibly the tenth time and for possibly the tenth time Flynn cuffed him lightly away. He might think of something he could do with the prawns and the fat. They waited.

Sally dipped her finger in the water and tried to draw a house and tree on the crate, but the sun sucked up her lines almost as quickly as she drew them. She gave up and talked cat language at Nebu. Nebu stretched, closed his eyes and ignored her.

A flight of seagulls scratched black marks on the flawless sky and wheeled towards the crate. They shrieked at Flynn and Sally as they scudded over the water, so low they carved brief lines in the surface with a carelessly lowered wing. A few gulls plopped heavily in the sea no more than an arm's length from Sally, but one bad-tempered tyrant puffed up his chest and ran across the water at them, squealing until they retreated.

Sally greeted the birds like old friends. While they scurried and bobbed about she seemed to feel nearly safe, and she waved at them. Nebu drew his paws under his body, apparently without moving, and watched the birds through eyes very nearly closed.

"See, I told you," Flynn said in strained triumph. "The gulls mean we're not far from shore."

An impetuous gull hovered over Flynn's bucket of prawns and put a single webbed foot on its rim. Immediately Nebu uncoiled from the crate and launched himself at the bird. The gull squawked and batted itself hastily into the air as Nebu collided with the bucket, sending it rolling. The gull escaped and Flynn shouted as he scrambled after the bucket, the fishing line, the bait, even the shells, as they all careered towards the edge. Flynn cuffed Nebu, but the cat swaggered to a far corner with a large green prawn in his mouth.

"We should see a lot of boats," Flynn said, as he refilled his bucket. "Anytime." He wished today was Saturday, or Sunday, when the sea was almost crowded. Everyone went to work on Tuesday.

Sally stroked Nebu and ran her tongue over her lips. "Nebu only wanted to catch breakfast. I'm hungry too."

"You want to eat a seagull?"

Sally shook her head.

"You can have anything from the bucket."

To Flynn's surprise, Sally studied the bucket and carefully picked up a prawn, tasted it, and took a small nibble.

"What's it like?"

Sally screwed up her face and held the prawn far from her mouth. Nebu swaggered to beneath her hand, sat back, raised a paw and gently eased the prawn from her fingers.

After a while the seagulls began to leave. They shrieked angrily at Flynn and kicked themselves into the air in small groups. A handful of birds hung high over the crate for a long time, but they drifted away. Sally watched the last gull disappear into the empty sky and, for no reason at all, she cried a little.

"Ah, don't do that, Sally," Flynn said. The sound of it was cutting at him. "Tell you what, we'll catch a fish."

Flynn pulled the fishing line from the bucket and impaled one of the prawns on the hook. He tossed the hook and the lead weight into the water and held the cork handle gently, so the sinker pulled the line slowly from the cork. The sinker and the prawn became smaller and smaller and less distinct until they disappeared.

And nothing happened.

"You've got to have patience."

That was what the old Dad said. And he had time to fish for yabbies in Guinnigan's Hole. Get a little piece of meat that was a little off, tie a bit of string around it, throw it in the water and wait. Sooner or later some stupid yabbie would grab at it with a claw and if you didn't jerk you could pull the creature all the way out of the waterhole. It would be too stupid to let go. But you don't do that in the city.

After a while Flynn pulled up the hook and found that the prawn had been taken. He put another prawn on the hook, using a little more care, dropping it in and waiting.

Sally suddenly kicked at the bucket, not enough to tip it over, just hard enough to move it.

"Don't do that!" Flynn shouted, slapping Sally lightly across the leg.

Sally slapped back. "Don't you hit me."

Flynn controlled himself. "What's wrong?"

"I'm bored. There's nothing to do."

"I can't help that, can I?"

Sally subsided into silence but she looked sour.

Flynn looked about him to get Sally's mind off things, then shaded his eyes and sat on the edge of the crate as if he was about to jump off. "See there, Sally! They're coming for us!"

Sally followed Flynn's quivering finger and tried to see what he was pointing at. There was nothing at all, but she didn't think Flynn was joking anymore.

"That white thing on the water. That's a sail."

There was a pinpoint of white on the horizon, so small it did not have a shape. It might have been a sail, or the edge of a wisp of cloud, or the sun bouncing off a wet rock.

Flynn waved at it, and shouted. But then he blinked and it wasn't there anymore. Flynn turned his back on the ocean and rubbed at the plank between his legs. He couldn't think of anything to say.

A little later the line jumped in Flynn's hands for perhaps half a second, then died. Flynn pulled up the hook, replaced the prawn and threw it back again.

"The sun's burning me up," said Sally.

She was sitting with her back to the sun, her arms pressed together in the shelter of her body and her knees drawn up to her chin. She looked as if she was trying to make herself so small that she would disappear. She was wearing only her old green swimming togs and the sun was sitting on her shoulders, slowly baking her.

Flynn looked at her and rubbed a worried finger hard over his teeth. Finally he took off his red shirt, looked at it and buttoned it at the neck. He sat the shirt on Sally's head like a small tent.

"Thank you," Sally said, but frowned. "You will get red."

Flynn peered over his shoulder at the mass of freckles across his back. "Not for a while." And then the

53

line twitched between his toes. He grabbed at the cork and felt something big and heavy in the water. "We've got something!"

He braced himself and began pulling. The fish pulled his arm straight and swam under the crate, catching the line against the hard edge of the wood. Flynn scrambled about on top to clear the line, ramming his knee into the bucket and almost sitting on Nebu. The line pulled and ran under the crate again, but Flynn was winding it in with increasing speed. Something flip-flopped on the water and Sally squealed and tried to catch it, but it danced beyond her fingers. Finally Flynn swung the one-kilogram ocean bream onto the top of the crate.

Nebu leapt at the thrashing fish and was cuffed aside by Flynn, who fought for almost a minute to pin it down. He managed to get the line under his heel for long enough to open his knife.

When the fish gave a last twitch on the planks Flynn withdrew his knife and washed it in the sea. His hands were shaking a little. But it was a good catch, almost thirty centimeters long, bigger than he'd ever caught with Dad. Wish he could see it now.

"What do we do with it?" said Sally, staring at the lifeless gray mound with a touch of horror.

"Well . . ." Flynn shrugged. "We eat it, of course." He cut off the head and gave it to Nebu, who took it to his corner, growled and started to chew. "See. Lovely stuff."

He cut a very small square from the belly of the fish and put it in his mouth. Rubber, salty and slippery. "It'll taste better when the sun cooks it a bit," he said.

By the middle of the afternoon Flynn could feel the sun in his skin and he was moving lips that were cracking, rigid, and didn't feel like they were his anymore. He thought of getting off the crate and swimming into it, under the shady planks, and resting in the cool still water where you could not see the endless horizon. But Sally would get frightened on the crate by herself and he would have to climb back again, scraping his knees and his chest on the planks.

He spent some time thinking about the friends he'd had at Parkes and still had at Bankstown. There was Dot at Parkes, and you could forget she was a girl because she was faster and stronger than almost anyone, and Ewen who'd sit on a fence and pretend he was a crow—maybe he really thought he was a crow. And Gary, who'd just come along and draw things in a notebook. And you'd lie under a tree and talk about things you could do and suck bitter grass.

That was very, very good. So why did it have to end?

Bankstown kids were always bigger and in a hurry.

And they lived in gangs. You get lonely until a gang picks you up. You come from Parkes? It might as well be the other side of Mars. But you can play Space Invaders and tell some jokes they haven't heard. So, there's Beetle, who's small. The Post Who Walks who's not, and Vithy, who's from Phnom Penh, and that's really on the other side of Mars. Sometimes when you're talking to Vithy he sounds like an old man, but he's no worse than the others. They have to compete. Like the time a train door was jammed open and you had to stand in the open space with your hands behind you and the first to grab was the loser. That wasn't funny.

"I'm awful thirsty," Sally said.

Nothing's funny anymore. Flynn turned lazily to his sister.

Her face was red and sweating and her tongue was moving very slowly across her lips. She had sounded a bit like a frog.

People die of thirst.

Flynn threw the sudden thought savagely from his mind. He tried to think of The Post as he almost fell out the train, or Vithy dancing under a spinning soccer ball, using everything but his arms to keep it in the air. He failed. The images came, blurred and faded. He even tried Dad, the back always turned to him, the head hunched under the desk lamp with Mum bustling about behind him. There was nothing to hang on to. Flynn stopped squirming and gave in.

People die of thirst.

But not yet. Not today. That's something that could happen in the future. Like starvation. We'll be picked up first. For sure.

"Try a pebble."

"What?"

"One of your pebbles. Just suck it." Flynn found a pebble in the bucket and passed it across.

Sally wrinkled her nose, but put the pebble in her mouth.

"Is it better?"

Sally shrugged. "Tase pishy," she said. But she kept the pebble in her mouth.

After a while Flynn tried a pebble himself. It worked a bit. His mouth thought it was a lollipop and sucked happily.

But he almost swallowed the pebble when he noticed a plume of smoke on the edge of the sea.

This time he watched it without speaking, even looking away to give it a chance to disappear like the sail. But it moved and it seemed to be increasing in size. Sally saw it for the first time just before it started to become a ship. She watched it, looked at Flynn and did not say anything either.

The smoke came from a single funnel which rose

with an infinite slowness from the water to show a faint derrick, a bridge, a lifeboat, and finally a black rusty hull.

"She's getting closer." Flynn took the pebble from his mouth. "This time she's coming for us. She'll pick us up." Flynn wasn't talking to Sally so much as persuading himself that this time the nightmare was going to end.

Sally smiled, but there was doubt in her eyes and Nebu kept on gnawing the skull of the fish and looked at the ship as if it were just another stretch of water.

The ship sailed towards the crate for the next half-hour. Flynn could see the ventilators round the funnel, the rust streaks below the anchor, the hot water being pumped into the sea, almost the name of the ship . . .

You know what she's going to do? thought Flynn. With my luck, she's just going to run us down. Gurgle, gurgle, chomp. It's aimed right at us. No. The captain's probably seen us already, and he's going to get so close he won't even have to lower a boat.

A suddenly happy thought came to Flynn. "You know, that ship might not be going to Sydney."

"I want to go home." And that was all Sally wanted. Nothing else.

"Oh, we will, we will. It will just take a little longer."

"I want to go home *now*."

"But what if that ship is going to Tahiti, or the

New Hebrides, or Fiji? We can't ask the captain to turn that huge ship around just for us. No, we stay on the ship as Very Important Guests and we have a look all over the ship, maybe even steer it—"

"Mum'll be worried."

"The Captain'll tell them where we are by radio." Flynn stopped and smiled. The Post would hear about us and he would be torn up in envy. That would be worth all the trouble that's waiting. And the Beetle would hear, and Vithy would accept this voyage as equal to his journey. Maybe even Dot will hear.

"Oh," said Sally.

"We'll go to Tahiti, and have a quick look around, coconuts and bananas, tribal feasts, and go home by plane . . ."

Flynn petered out. Once the broad cream wall of the bridge and the crew's quarters sat solidly behind the mast and cargo derricks, which meant that Flynn's slight fear was justified, that the ship was sailing straight up to the crate and might run it down if the crate was not seen. But the derrick had slid slowly to one side, there was a sliver of sea between the bridge and the mast, and that broad bridge was narrowing rapidly. The ship was going to pass them.

"Hey!" Flynn yelled. "Help!" His voice was being flooded with alarm. He shouted at the ship until his voice wheezed into a whimper and waved his arms so hard the crate rocked and turned, but the ship might as well have been a mirage. The front of the bridge had disappeared to be replaced by the full side view of an old, very rusty freighter with a ragged striped flag drooping at its stern.

"There's nobody there," Sally said.

Flynn could not see anyone on deck and the ship was a kilometer away but the beginning of stern perspective kicked him into action. He jumped to his feet to scream at the ship with what was left of his voice, to dance on the crate, to do anything at all to make someone on that ship see him. But the crate wasn't big enough to tolerate any violent movement. It tilted as Flynn leapt up, slewed as he sought his balance and bucketed under his weight. Flynn reeled around the planks, kicked Nebu from his corner, cannoned into Sally, slipped on the bream and hurtled into the sea.

Sally grabbed the spinning bucket even as she clutched the top of the pitching crate. She began to bawl from fright and pain, then she stopped and bit her lip.

An immense shadow was passing slowly under the crate.

EIGHT

FLYNN bubbled to the surface and saw Nebu floundering about in the water before he saw Sally and the crate.

"Flynn . . ." Sally was trying to shout in a whisper.

Flynn waved her down without looking at her. "All right, all right. I'll save your stupid cat again." He stroked towards Nebu.

"Flynn! There's a fish . . ."

Flynn stopped swimming an arm's length from the cat, and looked back at the crate as if he hadn't quite heard. "Fish?"

"Big fish. 'Normous fish in the water. Down there." Sally pointed at the quiet depth beneath Flynn.

Flynn stopped kicking and looked down. He saw something vast move lazily beneath the drifting columns of sunlight in the green, and felt very cold. He wanted to run in the water, to move his legs so fast that he would rise out of the sea and sprint across the surface of the crate. He wanted to scream . . .

Shh. You mustn't panic.

And Nebu kicked and screamed in the water, trying to reach him with those terrible sharp little claws. If he picked it up the cat would scratch, and he'd bleed and the blood would go into the water. Sharks can smell blood kilometers away and then they go mad . . .

And if he left the cat here in the water Sally would watch it drown, or get eaten. She'd never get over that.

The cat thrashed the water and coughed and shrieked and the shadow in the water slowly turned under the crate.

I can't . . .

Anyway, who said it was a shark?

And Flynn sucked in a deep breath, surged wildly to the cat and plucked it from the water by the scruff of its neck.

It could be only a porpoise.

Flynn held the cat over his head, so the tail whipped under his nose and the dripping fur blinded him, and stroked with one arm, carefully sidekicking towards the crate.

"Watch the fish, Sally," he called. He was not going to call it Shark.

"It is still there."

The cat stopped squirming, and was silent, drooping limply from Flynn's grip. It was incredibly heavy. Its right rear clawed paw was resting on his cheek and he couldn't lift it away. He rolled his head into the water and stared at the deep water, but he could not see the shadow any more.

"You are swimming the wrong way!" Sally's voice, from one side.

He blinked his eyes clear and swam towards a watery glimpse of something square. "Where's the fish?"

Silence.

"Where's the fish?"

"Behind you."

Flynn was swimming faster now, and he wanted so much to throw the cat away.

"Where? How far—" He felt his toe brush something, opened his mouth to scream, kicked desperately and saw a brown strand of seaweed tangled in his foot.

"It's getting closer," Sally said from somewhere above him.

Suddenly the cat squirmed, scratched and was gone. He dropped his arm into the water and brushed his knuckles against the wood of the crate. He didn't bother looking for the empty side this time, just kicked furiously and butterflyed himself to the top of the crate.

He sat on the crate, trembling in the sun, for a long time.

"Are you all right?" Sally asked.

Flynn jerked his head up. " 'Course I'm all right. I'm not a sissy." He had been seeing horrifying visions of what might have happened, what still might happen. An old crate is a very fragile defense against shark attack. "Um, is it still down there?"

Sally looked into the water with the idle curiosity of a visitor to an aquarium. She doesn't know, Flynn thought. She just doesn't know.

"No . . ." Sally said. "Oh. Yes, it's still there." She sounded a little disappointed.

Flynn nodded and lifted his eyes to the dirty little freighter, now showing a distant stern and crawling away to the horizon. He felt old pebbles in his stomach.

"It was too far away, wasn't it, Flynn?"

It was just too much. He could look down and see that his hands were still shaking. His one hope of rescue had pretended he wasn't there and sailed past him, leaving him alone in the middle of the ocean, and a great shark had swum up from its depths, missing him by the breadth of a finger. It was still out there, waiting. And that nasty, cool little girl was carrying on as if he'd had a gravel rash.

Flynn turned to Sally in anger. "What do you know? It's too far away, they're all too far away."

"What do you mean?"

"Look around, stupid." Flynn waved his arms. "There's nothing on this bloody ocean but us."

They both became silent and looked at the water, from the gleaming rim, the scudding surface shadows of distant zephyrs, the stray captured cloud, to the circular ripples made by the crate. Eventually the wake of the ship would spread across the water and nudge the crate, and after that the ship might never have been there.

Flynn wanted to curl into a tiny ball and suck his thumb and bawl. He did not want to be a hero, a space traveller, a pirate, anymore. It was all too hard. He just wanted to be a small boy, and it was unfair to expect him to be anything else.

But Sally stopped staring at the ocean and looked at Flynn with haunted eyes. "Nobody is ever going to save us?" she said, very softly.

Flynn watched Sally's mouth begin to quiver, her eyes fill and her face change as she felt helpless, hollow fear for the first time in her life.

She is only five years old.

So what? What's the point of protecting her, giving her everything in icing sugar? She's got to grow up.

Sally looked up through her tears at Flynn, hoping for a bit of hope to push back a sudden feeling of sickness. "Someone's going to find us, Flynn? Sometime?"

Flynn turned away from Sally.

"No," he said.

NINE

THE first time Flynn had to look after Sally was the time of the fire. And he'd hated it.

It had been so hot and dry for so long that nobody could remember exactly when it had rained properly. Showers were down to one minute and the shower water went to the vegetable garden. Guinnigan's Hole was still deep enough to swim in, but it was too much of a risk to swing over it and drop. The remains of a bullock cart now tumbled in the mud, but there were only two wheels left and it could not be moved. A few boys came to the Hole every day, not to swim so much as to see what the receding water would reveal.

Out of the Hole, people slept on verandahs and sat in the shade and waited for the fire. It had to come.

When it came roaring out of a small valley nobody was ready for its size and power. Dad disappeared with forty men on trucks and came back alone, black and tired, with a hessian bag slung over his shoulder. An old house had burst into flame four hundred meters away.

"The others are coming," he said. "Get out of the house."

Mum grabbed Sally and Flynn and ran towards the Hole as a tall wall of flame swept through the trees around the house. "What are you going to do?" she shouted. "You can't save the house!"

"You have to do something!" Dad yelled back.

He pulled bucket after bucket from the well, jammed the downpipes, flooded the gutters, threw water at the old weatherboard walls, soaked his hessian bag and walked towards the fire. Like facing a tiger with a pin.

The fire blew an angry roar from the trees to the belt of long yellow grass before the house, and ignited it instantly. Smoke billowed about the man as he flailed at the blaze, then he was surrounded by fire and retreating towards the house.

A curl of smoke stung Flynn's eyes. "I want to help," he said. He was surprised. He didn't think that was what he had wanted to say at all, he was too frightened.

Mum reached for his shoulder, found it and brought her face down to his, suddenly a hard, white mask with no lips and whisps of ash hair curling over the forehead. "You can help. You just stay here, just here, and look after Sally . . ."

"Aw, Mum."

"Now stay here! I don't have time to argue." And she was gone. Sally clung to his leg and bawled.

Mum waded through the fire and Dad stopped in surprise for perhaps half a swing, and he nodded at her. Flame flickered across their faces and she was shouting at him. A branch screamed and fell in a long twisting, blazing arc to the grass and it exploded.

Suddenly Mum was alone, swinging at a howling ring of fire with the hessian bag and Dad was running—actually running!—to safety behind her.

Sally looked up at Flynn and bawled. Flynn picked her up and held her at face height. "If you don't shut up," he told her, "I'll throw you in the fire."

Sally stopped and fingered the sudden tears on her brother's cheeks, then kept on bawling.

Mum was out of the long grass now, standing on the three meters of worn stubble between the fire and the front wall of the house. The black hessian in her hand was burning, the window sill behind her was burning, just about everything was burning or about to burn.

The fire hurled itself from the trees, from the grass, from the stubble at Mum and the house and Mum had even stopped swinging at it. She was just standing there with her shoulders hunched and her face black.

"I'll kill him!" Flynn shouted uselessly. "I will, I'll kill him!"

The fire roared and clanked back at him.

Clanked?

Some sort of dragon was chewing through the flames towards Mum, coughing, lurching, glaring, snorting as it moved. And Mum had gone mad. She was grinning at it, waving it on.

For an instant the smoke swirled clear and Dad was riding the dragon, pushing it into flames as high as his shoulder. And behind him the flames twisted and coughed and became vast pillars of thick black smoke.

Dad on the tractor, towing the scarifier behind him. Breaking the fury of the fire.

Then a white-bearded man with a chainsaw started felling burning scrub and trees. Five men and a water truck stopped near the house and turned the black smoke to dirty gray. The bushfire was turned back and after a while it could be ignored to roar away down a gully. Dad jumped from the now black tractor, picked up Mum, put her down, put his arm across her shoulder and laughed.

Then he looked at Flynn in the shade of Guinnigan's Tree, frowned and walked towards him. Flynn tried to wipe the water from his eyes with the back of his arm and Sally stopped bawling with a sniffle.

"What's up, son?" Dad squatted before him.

Flynn waved his hand uselessly. "I thought—you were running away."

"Ah. Doesn't matter. We beat it, didn't we?"

Flynn shook his head. "No. You stopped the fire, Mum stopped the fire. I didn't do anything. Just looked."

"No, Flynn," Dad rubbed Sally's head and she tried to bite a finger. "You looked after Sally. *We* beat it. All of us. Let's go and have a drink."

T E N

Flynn could hear Sally behind him. Not crying or anything, just talking slowly, softly.

". . . that's all right. Don't worry . . ."

He turned on the crate to look at his little sister.

Sally was sitting cross-legged with Nebu a shivering little ball on her lap. She was feeding him a prawn as she spoke to him.

"It's all right, Nebu," she was saying. "Don't be afraid. I'll look after you."

Flynn closed his eyes. He swallowed twice and breathed slowly for a few seconds. He opened his eyes again, looked at Sally, and his lips moved.

"I'm sorry, Sally," he said.

Sally looked up from Nebu. "Okay."

"I was just a bit angry back there. You know, the ship and the shark and everything. We'll get home all right. Don't worry."

Sally actually smiled. She stroked Nebu. "See, I told you," she said to the cat.

Flynn shrugged for something more to say. "Well . . ." He remembered Dad with a wall of fire at his back and a burnt old bag in his hand. You have to do something.

"Well, we can't sit around doing nothing anymore. It's no good just waiting for someone to rescue us. We'll have to do something."

"What?"

She would ask that. All right, what?

Flynn moved a little and felt a plank shift under him. He lifted himself, crabbed sideways and worked the plank with his fingers. He could move it perhaps a centimeter from side to side and half a centimeter up and down. Maybe he could work it free completely.

"What are you doing?"

"Shh. I'm thinking."

There were nine planks across the top of the crate, nailed to two solid cross pieces at each end. Remove this one and you would not be weakening the crate. Much. The plank was right in the middle of the top of the crate. If you could take the plank off you could jam the bucket into the space and stop it from rolling over the edge.

But what would you do with the plank?

Paddle with it.

Hit the shark with it, if it ever decides to come up from the deep.

Just have it in your hands so you can wave it at boats.

Flynn pulled the knife out of the bucket and began to work on the wood around the nails. He felt better already. Doing something was far better than just sitting there and thinking.

Or just sitting there and being the world's worst creep.

Shut up.

"What are you doing?" Sally said.

"I'm making a paddle."

"What for?"

"To paddle home."

Sally looked at the distant horizon. "All that way?"

A piece of the blade splintered off. "Shut up," he said.

"Can I help?"

"Later." Flynn put the knife away and began to pull the plank up, jerking the wood hard and suddenly against the nails.

"You'll break the box," Sally said.

"No," Flynn said and ignored her.

Sally pulled her feet up and watched in worried silence, sucking her knee. Nebu stalked into her shade and stared at Flynn like a marble bookend, still steaming in the heat.

A split appeared in the plank, running from one of the nails. "Aah—!" Flynn began, then he realized that the split would give him a better handle to the paddle. It would be fine if the split could be persuaded to run off the side rather than splitting straight. He examined the grain in the plank, shrugged and pulled at the wood until it jerked clear of the nail. It cracked in a long crescent to the edge.

He hefted the free piece of wood and thought about lashing the knife to one end with fishing line to form a spear. Later. He didn't want to create another split in the plank at the remaining nail so he inserted the knife blade under the plank and levered.

A curl of hair was lifted from his forehead, held loose in the air and allowed to flop back in place. Flynn felt the touch of cool after the puff of wind had swept on. He turned his head to catch the next puff but it never came.

He shrugged, and smiled at Sally. "That was nice."

"What?"

"The wind."

"Oh. It's hot."

Flynn returned to the blade and the plank, but a little later he lifted his head and looked at the ocean before him. It didn't look like a sheet of glass anymore. There was air moving over the surface, brushing patches of fast ripples across the water.

What do you do out here in a storm?

Shut up.

Flynn jammed four fingers of his free hand into the space left by the split and pulled with his entire upper body until his shoulders and back began to hurt. The head of the nail, red with rust, folded like a rose and the end of the plank came clear.

Sally looked down at the dark slot in the middle of the crate. "It's full of water," she said.

" 'Course it is," Flynn breathed heavily and rubbed at the groove the knife had left in his right hand. "It hasn't got an end, remember." He caught the look in Sally's eyes and smiled. "It's all right. We won't sink."

Sally looked at the water beneath her and lifted her head. "I forgot."

Flynn lifted the plank to shoulder height, bending the two big nails which held down the other end. He ran his hand down the curved edge. "Now, how's that for a paddle? The next ship goes past, we'll chase it."

"Can I paddle?"

"It's too big."

"You've got two paddles. A big one and a little one." Sally pointed.

"Oh yes, go ahead. Just don't lose it. I can't jump into the sea after it." Flynn had just remembered the big fish, still down there in the deep.

Sally picked up the split piece of wood by its point and began to wave it about in the water. "Where do I paddle?"

A light patch of breeze tickled the side of Flynn's face and he turned towards it. He felt as if his face was being washed by the air. He waited for the breeze to pass and then turned back to nod at the dipping sun. "That way."

Sally paddled enthusiastically for a few seconds and the crate began to turn. Flynn placed his foot against the partly raised plank and pushed, until it was held upright at the end of the crate by the bent nails. Like a very small telegraph pole. The breeze returned, and this time it stayed, no more than a touch of warm air, but it was there.

Sally hit the water with the paddle in anger. "It won't go anywhere. Just goes round in circles."

"Now wait a sec." Flynn frowned at the plank, old wood lightly coated with salt. A pole with the sun at the top.

There was something . . .

"Sally? Can I have that paddle back?"

"Why?"

"Oh come on!"

Sally passed the paddle back and sulked. Flynn cut the hook and sinker from the fishing line and dropped them in the bucket. They might catch the cat instead, and it would serve the thieving animal right. He cut the point off Sally's paddle and used the fishing line to lash it high on the upright plank.

Sally cocked her head and stroked . "What's *T* for?"

Flynn tested the firmness of the lashing and sat on his heels. "What *T*?"

Sally pointed at the plank and the paddle. "That *T*."

"Oh. It's for Trouble, if you don't leave me alone. Can I have my shirt back?"

Sally took it off her head and handed it to Flynn without a word.

Flynn undid the button at the neck and hung the shirt on the paddle where it lifted a little and swayed like a man staggering.

"It's a scarecrow!" Sally shouted. "Ships are going to see us!"

"Maybe. But we're not waiting." He tied the fishing line to a bottom corner of the shirt, took it fairly tautly to a corner plank, across to the other corner, then to the other bottom corner of the shirt, where he tied it. Then all the way back and back again, trebling the line.

Flynn felt a little like being trapped in a cage of nylon lines, but the old red shirt was filling with air and the wood began to creak.

"We're sailing," said Sally in wonder.

"Trying to," said Flynn, running a line from a rear corner of the crate to the top of the upright plank and back to the other corner, and back again. He was trying to remember how yachts were rigged and trying to work out what a wind would do to his funny little sail.

After a while he could not think of anything else to do, so he sat back and watched his shirt bag an armful of air and hold it. At least it looks like we're going somewhere, he thought. But it's really not much better than a paddle. Someone on a ship might just see the shirt, now that it's up high, but it has about as much hope of moving this dirty great box as a handkerchief on a pier. Or a pin against a tiger . . .

Yeah, Dad, the old Dad would like it.

But Sally was happy. If she thought the crate was moving she wouldn't be so frightened, she might even forget what sort of cruddy kid he'd been an hour ago.

Sally moved a little closer to the sail, so that she was sitting in its shade. She looked at the water by her side and Flynn realized that she was staring at the seaweed drifting around the crate. She must be able to work out that the crate was not going anywhere at all.

"Flynn . . ."

Flynn sighed. Sally had worked it out far too soon. "Yes."

"The big fish."

"Oh." He was trying to forget about it. Was it coming? He thought briefly about the little knife in the bucket. "Where?"

"It's gone."

Some invisible giant took his foot off Flynn's chest, "Really?" He peered into the water and the crate tilted.

"I can't see it anywhere," said Sally. "I think it has got bored."

"Good. Beauty."

"And we are nearly going speedy."

"Um. Yes, of course. I told you . . . Hey!"

78

A strand of seaweed, a long ribbon of leather bubbles and brown leaves, was sliding very slowly along the side of the crate. And an old piece of cork bobbed gently to their rear.

Except it wasn't the rear of an old crate anymore. It was the stern of a boat, with a bow, a mast and a sail. And the boat was creaking, straining as it pushed through the ocean.

"We're really moving," Flynn said in astonishment.

"You're clever," Sally said, and got to her knees and kissed him.

"Well . . ." Flynn was more surprised by the kiss than the knowledge that he had made a crate sail. For as long as he could remember, Sally had been the enemy, the teller of tales, the pest you had to drag along, the little girl that just wouldn't be impressed no matter what you did. Now, it was all different.

"You're nearly as clever as Daddy."

Flynn shook his head. At that moment he could build a rocket to the moon, or chase after that cowardly shark with the knife between his teeth. He could do anything.

He pointed beneath the swelling red sail, past the square bow, at the shining horizon. "Home is that way. And we're going to sail there. All the way!"

Flynn and Sally looked at each other.

And laughed.

ELEVEN

No, it had not been war all the time. There was the time of the accident. You forget about things like that. Maybe you want to forget about things like that.

Bankstown, last year: testing The Post's new bicycle. The Post, Flynn and always Little Sal, four years old. Little Sal was supposed to sit on the gutter and watch Flynn and The Post demonstrate the finer points of riding. But Sally rarely sat still and was never quiet. When The Post rode steadily past sitting on the bar and facing backwards she wanted to know why he wanted to ride like that.

She was told to shut up.

Flynn managed to cover one meter in three minutes in a feat of slow riding which had him standing perfectly still for twenty-five seconds—despite Sally hopping round and round the bike singing "Oranges and Lemons."

"I didn't know you could ride like that," The Post said.

"I can even drive a tractor."

Sally looked up brightly, eager to join the boys. "I can catch frogs."

"Yeah, that's fine," The Post said. "You're all on about the farm again. Why didn't you stay there?"

Flynn shrugged. "I didn't want to leave. They made me. No, Mum was crying a lot. Dad made all of us leave."

"Why?"

"I dunno."

"Well, you're here now. Stop whining all the time." The Post climbed on the bike and rode off slowly, pedalling with one foot, steering with one finger.

"Sometimes I liked the farm," Sally said wistfully.

"You can remember it then?"

"I had a big rock under a tree. And I played horse on it and climbed it and slid down it. But you and Daddy shot it once. You shouldn't have done that."

"Oh." Flynn could remember empty cans on a useless gray rock and Dad was showing him how to fire a gun without dislocating a shoulder. Flynn knew he'd been in the army because he'd seen photos, but Dad wouldn't talk about that at all. The only time he'd seen the gun was when Dad had shot a sheep. It was a rare moment that had led to the shooting of Sally's rock. "We weren't shooting at the rock, y'know. Just the cans."

The Post was riding back towards them, whooping like a movie Indian and leaning so far out that he could pluck paper from the pavement.

"It wasn't a rock. It was a horse, Skoowby, and he's gone now."

"Ah, come on Sally—"

Then he was on his feet and shouting.

For one instant everything seemed to freeze. There was The Post hurtling towards them on his wildly tilting bike. He would have passed them but his sock had caught in the chain and he was off-balance. His whooping had changed to a panicked scream and Sally sat on the curb before the bike, her hand drifting up in a very fragile defense. And now Flynn was in the air, high over Sally and reaching for the bike.

Flynn struck the front wheel of the bike and The Post's shoulder hit him in the jaw and Sally began shouting and the back wheel lofted like a frisky pony. The Post shouted "What . . . !"

And everything began to fall and skid and buckle. Flynn spun to the road with one arm around The Post and the other hand grasping something of metal and rubber. His foot hit something sharp and the bike unfolded about him. It wasn't a bicycle, it was a thousand bicycles and it would never stop clanging, rasping, banging and punching at him.

But it did. He heard Sally crying, but it was a low cry, so it couldn't be too bad. He moved and gasped. It seemed that every bone in his body was broken and he was definitely dying. He listened to the ticking of a wheel spinning past his ear. Someone crawled painfully across his chest and he shouted in anger. He threw parts of the bike from him and half-rose to face The Post. "You're a great nit, Walker! The greatest cruddy nit ever!"

The Post didn't seem to hear. He picked up his bike by its scarred handlebars, looked at the tilted pedal, buckled wheel, broken light, twisted mudguard and the scratches. "Why'd you do that? You've wrecked me bike."

"Your bike?" Flynn took a step towards the bike and kicked at the spokes of the intact wheel. "You nearly hit my sister. Get out!"

The Post swung his bike away from Flynn and paused, deciding whether to fight Flynn. Then he saw Sally and sadly wheeled his bike away.

Flynn hobbled over to Sally and reached down. Sally ignored his hand and jumped up.

"You okay?"

She nodded. "We better go home." She kept looking at the blood on his knees, arms and even the face.

Flynn tried to walk easily ahead of Sally but the pain in his right foot and the spreading bruises turned his walk into a lurch with many stops for air. After a while Sally took his hand and put it on her shoulder. She became his walking stick. They were able to move a little faster and a little easier, but some of his blood brushed off on her.

Unfortunately they were first seen by Dad.

Dad half-rose from his chair and his face darkened as he saw Sally's torn dress and the blood on her head.

"My God, boy, what have you done to her?"

But Little Sally stepped between Flynn and Dad and shouted. "You just leave Flynny alone! It's not fair."

And Dad stopped rising, with sudden astonishment across his face. He looked at Sally, at Flynn and at Sally again. He sat down.

"All right," he said. "What happened?"

Afterwards, when Flynn had sat in a bath for almost half an hour, and been attacked by Mum with iodine and bandages, and couldn't move much at all, he called Sally.

She skipped into his room. "You look awful."

"Yeah, I know. Look, ah, I'm sorry I shot at your horse."

She shrugged. "Aah, it's only a rock."

And he'd forgotten that.

T W E L V E

FLYNN thought about the accident for a long part of the afternoon, while the breeze rose, pulling the fishing lines taut and strumming them like a guitar. First he thought about Sally and without a word reached out and scrabbled his fingers in her hair. She beat him off with a cross frown, as the crate began to slope down slightly towards the straining shirt. They had to move towards the stern to bring up the bow and the crate began to sail a little faster. But the faster the crate went the harder it was to keep it on course. Flynn had to act as the crate's rudder and the only way to do it was to sit in the stern and kick in the water, all the time watching for shadows in the water.

Then he thought about Dad. He could remember him at the farm a little before the family had left, and he hadn't changed then. They were walking round the farm remembering things. They visited Guinnigan's Hole and looked up at the place Flynn had fallen from to plummet into the deep black water. Now you could run across the bottom. Dad had patted Flynn's shoulder and they had wandered back to inspect the tractor. After the fire it had never been the same and it had at last stopped, a scorched derelict in a patch

of yellow stubble. Dad was going to fix it up sometime. Flynn had shown Dad his fort, a cluster of rocks
and a ti-tree on a hillock, where he'd stood off Indians,
bandits, tanks and space invaders. And Dad talked
about the smugglers' cave he'd had as a boy, with
mysterious bones, a view of the sea and a torch that
wouldn't work. They'd found a dead sheep in a far
paddock and buried it together before they'd gone
home, more or less as mates.

But this same Dad a while later had seen Flynn and
Sally come tottering in from the accident and instantly
blamed Flynn. "My God, boy, what have you done
to her?" As if Flynn had beaten her up, or pushed her
off a cliff or thrown rocks at her. Some mates!

Flynn kicked savagely at the water.

Suddenly he was kicking his right foot into a ball
of soft rubber and his toes were tingling. He jerked
himself clear of the water with a frightened yelp and
brushed quivering fragments of transparent matter
from his foot.

"Jellyfishes," he said angrily. And forgot about
Dad, the farm and the accident as his foot turned red.

The crate thudded gently into something soft and
Sally began to count.

"There's an awful lot," she said when she ran out
of numbers.

An endless parade of huge, silent mushrooms

drifted past or beneath the crate, long white trailers hanging far beneath them until they disappeared in the deepening blue.

"What do they taste like?" Sally asked.

Flynn was banging his foot on the crate. "They're poisonous. Look at my foot."

Sally looked. "They're nasty."

"Well, I tell you, I'm not going to put my foot in the water with those about." The crate began to drift sideways.

"I'm hungry."

"There's that fish I caught, isn't there?" Flynn scratched his foot.

"Yuck."

"There's nothing else, is there?"

Sally was quiet while the wind caught the sail and straightened the crate. "I know," she said softly. "I was just saying it."

Flynn let his foot alone and smiled at Sally. He squeezed her hand. She deserved at least that. "Look, we're going home now, look at that sail. We'll get home and we'll have roast beef and carrots and gravy and peas and potatoes and pumpkin and—"

"I don't like pumpkin."

"Okay, scratch pumpkin. And then we'll have strawberries and cream . . ."

"Ice-cream."

"Ice-cream."

"What will we have next?"

"Um. Biscuits and cheese?"

"And coffee."

"Coffee?"

"Like Mum and Dad." She looked a little wistful.

"I didn't know you liked coffee."

"This is different. We're playing make-believe."

"Oh. Yes."

They sat on the crate for a while and looked at the sea and didn't talk and thought about things.

Like The Post. Since the accident they were almost mortal enemies. The bike had been repaired as new apart from a few scratches. Flynn had to think hard to remember where his injuries had been. But he and The Post wouldn't speak to each other, wouldn't play together and kept out of each other's way. It was a stupid feud. What The Post had almost done to Sally was very small compared to what Flynn was doing to her now.

If they got back . . .

When they got back Flynn would see how The Post was these days. After all, they had been friends. If The Post didn't want to know him, well at least he'd tried . . .

Flynn suddenly yelped and arched his back as the soft wind tossed a spread of spray onto his back. He watched the wind stretch the shirt, filling it like a sack of pumpkins, flapping the arms. Nebu hissed at the ocean and nuzzled into Sally's downwind side.

"It's cold," Sally complained.

"Doesn't matter. Look." Flynn was pointing to the bow of the crate in excitement.

At the leading edge of the crate there was a low hump in the water.

"We're really moving. Ripping along," Flynn almost whispered. As if the wind might hear and stop blowing or he might wake up. It was like making up tales for Sally and finding that the wizard with the whirlwind in his hat really existed.

"Yes." Sally was unimpressed this time. "I'm cold." It was all right moving across a sea as quiet as an old river with the sun to keep you warm, but this was bumpy, the wind gave you goose pimples. It was almost as scary as last night, when the sea took you away.

"Yes, but we're going home!"

"You said that before."

Flynn subsided. "Yes, but we're going home faster now. We'll get there in no time at all. Look at the water."

"Yes. I s'pose." Sally had been out on the sea for too long, too long without shelter and food, too long without water. She needed more than faint movement in the water and a grin from her brother to encourage her now.

"We'll get there," Flynn said emptily.

Nebu gnawed furtively at the fish.

The wind steadied and blew the crate across the ocean for the rest of the afternoon. And for the rest of the afternoon Flynn steered the crate with his legs and faced the spray. His feet became white and wrinkled, the edge of the crate gouged a trench across the bottom of his legs, the sun burned his chest, and the wind chilled him. But above all this he was feeling very tired.

Sally lay flat on the crate and missed most of the spray while catching the warmth of the slowly sinking sun. She might have fallen asleep for an hour or two, and Flynn did not disturb her.

Towards the end of the afternoon a rumpled rim of dark cloud slid over the eastern horizon. Flynn watched it grow slowly, spreading like mud flung into clear water. He tried to persuade himself that it meant nothing at all.

Then Sally rolled over and Flynn caught her before she tumbled into the water. She looked at Flynn in happy puzzlement, then emptily at the sea and the sky.

"It hasn't changed." Sally had been dreaming of coloring clowns beside a fire and her eyes brimmed.

"We're a lot closer, Sal, really," Flynn said quickly.

Sally shook her head at the endless water. "We're

not going anywhere. There's just waves and waves. We're not going to—"

"Just hang on. I'm going to have a look." Flynn took his feet out of the water and turned. Nothing but sea. But you couldn't see more than a hundred meters from this height because of the waves.

Flynn looked from the dissolving face of his sister to the rolling cloud and back. At that moment he was more afraid than ever before in his life.

Sally might die tonight.

Tonight there was going to be a storm. It might be a very bad storm and it was going to be cold, very cold. She hasn't had anything to drink or eat for a day and a half. And she's been burnt by the sun and she's been frightened all the time. Even through the games we play. If she doesn't have something to cling to she might give up tonight. She's only five.

He slowly raised himself to a kneeling position and the crate bucketed slightly.

Sally blinked her eyes clear and gulped. "What are you doing?"

"Just don't move." Flynn raised his right knee to his chin and prepared his face.

He was going to get to his feet, look at the sea and grin and shout, "I can see land!" no matter what he saw. Something to keep Sally going, no matter how bad this night was going to be.

He raised his body and the crate tilted. He bent over

as he spread his feet, balancing the crate in the waves. He looked down at Sally and smiled, and she stared back at him.

He straightened, saw wave upon wave upon wave, and grinned and said, "I can see land . . ."

And a moment later he shouted in amazement, "I can!"

T H I R T E E N

FLYNN swayed on the hard wood of the crate and was a little frightened as the sea rolled around him. As far as he could see the waves slid together, flattened, surged apart in a constantly shifting pattern of foam-speckled dark green water.

But there was something else.

Through the turbulent hills and valleys of the ocean there was a black humped line that lifted into view from behind a wave, dipped behind another, appeared again, dipped . . . But it did not change. It was always a low peak, a short level line and a hollow, as if a great mouse had nibbled at it. Water does not behave like that. It flows, it drifts before the wind, it swells, wallows, ridges, changes every single moment.

Only land does not change.

"I can see it!" Flynn repeated in a pant, staring hard at the mouse-nibble to prevent it from escaping. "That's home!" He pointed across the sea.

"Let me have a look!" Sally scrambled to her feet.

And the crate careered round in a half circle, canting dangerously and with the shirt flagging in the wind. Nebu screeched in fright.

"Get down!" Flynn threw his feet out from under

him, pulling Sally down as he dropped. The crate creaked and rocked but eventually began to steady. Flynn kicked desperately to get the wind behind the shirt.

"I'm sorry," Sally said.

"Ah, why did you have to . . ." Flynn started shouting, then stopped. "That's all right. Just be careful. We're getting there."

"What did you see?"

"A cliff." Flynn thought a bit. "Or a hill."

Sally cocked her head and looked at Flynn. "You're only saying that."

Flynn remembered his original plan and felt a sliver of guilt. But it wasn't fair to accuse him now. "It's there. It's really there."

"Why can't I see it?"

Before he would have told Sally it was too dangerous for her to get up high and look, and didn't she trust him? But this was different. "All right. I'll show you. Get up on my back."

Sally climbed onto Flynn's shoulders and he straightened his back and the crate began to bucket and slide sideways. Flynn tried to ignore the crate and even rose to his knees for a handful of frightened seconds. He lowered quickly as the crate turned into the wind.

"No," Sally said, as she got off Flynn's back and

sat on the crate, hugging her knees. "I can't see anything."

Flynn kicked the crate back on course. "It's there.
I tell you it's there."

"How far?"

Flynn thought. "Oh—ah—maybe two kilometers." Maybe six, or eight, or even ten, but two
sounds better.

"It's not there." Sally nodded sadly.

"What do you want? Why would I want to tell you
I can see things that aren't there?"

"Because I'm a little girl. People tell make-believe
things to little girls."

Flynn looked at Sally for a long time. This little
girl he didn't know at all. "Look, it's there. Or I think
it's there. If it's make-believe then I'm fooled too.
You didn't see it because I couldn't get you high
enough, but it's there. I think I saw something solid
like a hill, and it's maybe eight kilometers away."

"You said two keeyomeets."

"Closer to eight."

She looked at him, frowned and for some peculiar
reason she began to smile. "Okay."

"It wasn't there before, so we are going towards
it, not going away like in the beginning. But we are
not going to get there until very late at night. Okay?"

"Okay," she said.

They were still smiling at each other when the sparkling of the water dimmed and the wind chilled their backs. The sun had dropped behind the sail, giving their skins a crimson glow, but losing much of its warmth. Flynn stopped kicking the water and looked up into the wind to see that the dark cloud was now a great arch over the eastern horizon. A long gray veil was being trailed from the cloud to the sea.

"There's your glass of water," Flynn said in brittle cheerfulness.

Sally, lying on her stomach on the crate and squeezing the warmth out of the wood, said nothing.

The wind dropped a little as the sun slid its lower rim beneath the sail, and they felt a last few minutes of comfortable heat. Then the sun touched the water and began to dissolve into the sea and the sky. Flynn could amost reach out and touch a rolling wave of crimson water as the cloud banks rippled and blazed in silence.

Sally sat up to watch the sunset and held her hands out as if to warm them by the dying fire. Then the sun had gone and the color of the day began to leech from the sky, leaving Flynn with the darkness of his thoughts.

It's going to be a bad night, when the storm hits. It's cold now, the moment the sun goes, and it's going to get far colder tonight. We're going to be so wet, there's going to be spray and waves just rolling over the crate. We'll get wet and the wind'll blow and we'll freeze. Really freeze. And we might get tipped off the crate and drown. Might? Probably will. What can you do?

Flynn watched the towering cloud tumbling towards him and closed his eyes.

And just suppose you and Sally can stand the cold and the wind and the water. And just suppose you and the crate make it to the shore. Well, most of the shore north of Sydney is cliffs and rocks. You'll get thrown on the rocks by the storm that gets you there, and that will be that. You forgot about that, didn't you?

So what do you do, Dad?

No, you're on your own. What you do is just hang on and wait. There's nothing else.

Flynn did not consider taking down the shirt.

Flynn was glad when the last traces of sunlight faded from the sky. It meant that he couldn't see the approaching storm. It was cold, dark and miserable. The wind altered its tone and Nebu pressed against Flynn's side and began to miaow plaintively.

A few minutes later he saw a gray line in the water, as if a great curtain was being trailed across the waves. He became alarmed by it without knowing what it was.

Then he knew.

"It's the storm," he said, very quietly.

F O U R T E E N

SALLY was stroking Nebu, but the cat was erect and trembling.

Flynn could see seams stitched in the water, small fast ripples behind the scudding line, then a flying shadow.

The storm hit the crate like an axe.

The fragile little mast creaked, the shirt ballooned and tried to break away from singing fishing lines. The crate slewed and tilted, rolling Sally to the edge. Sally cried out and clutched at Flynn's back and the wood. Flynn caught her arm and kicked at the water in an effort to regain control. His legs were hot and heavy with exhaustion, moving slowly now and he watched them as if they belonged to someone else. The wind was full of flying spray and was colder than he had imagined it could be. It was roaring, a huge and angry animal.

"Hang on!" Flynn shouted. "Hang on."

Nebu turned to face the wind and sank his claws deep in the timber. He crouched, flattened his ears and closed his eyes. He was no longer mewing.

Behind the wind came the waves. New waves, bigger and faster, with white peaks jostling the crate in a terrible hurry. Flynn's kicking became an agony, then useless. The crate turned, heaved and wallowed, pushing the sail sideways and back on its mast. But now it wasn't a sail or a mast anymore. It was a flapping, sodden red shirt on two staggering sticks on a dangerously creaking crate. The shirt began to tear.

"I'm scared . . ." Sally was biting at her lips.

Flynn squeezed her arm. He couldn't trust his voice anymore.

One of the lines holding the shirt snapped with a loud *ping!* and the shirt lifted from the crate like a wildly waving man. Flynn swung his feet out of the water and reached for the shirt as another line snapped. The wet shirt cracked in the wind, lashed Flynn's arm and jerked the mast into the water. Flynn held his arm for a moment, rocking back and forwards until the pain subsided, then fished his shirt from the foam of a crest. The mast and crosstree were gone.

Sally looked at him, her mouth moving as if she were saying something, but there was no sound. Her eyes were glittering.

He touched her shoulder and shouted, "Lie down," over the howl of the wind. They were too high on this rickety crate. Nebu had the right idea.

Sally lay on the crate, on one side of the missing plank. The cleft now sluiced rectangular waves over the top of the crate, making it seem that the crate was breaking into two in the surging water.

Flynn looked at Sally and felt a block of ice in his stomach. He couldn't swallow and he wanted to lie on the crate, close his eyes and whimper.

But he managed a chilly smile for Sally. Sally looked away.

He squeezed some of the water from the shirt and slowly put it on. It was cold, it clung to his body like a thick stain, but it kept the wind from his skin.

He lay beside Sally and tried to get used to the twisting, pitching darkness. Somewhere out there a great angry animal was howling at them, becoming wilder as the storm grew. The waves slammed against the crate's sides, turning it, heaving it about like a matchbox in a bath, hurling spray into the air and forcing flat swells through the cleft.

Flynn and Sally were as wet as if they were swimming in the storm and very much colder. Flynn held Sally to the top of the crate but his fingers had lost the feeling of the wood.

"I'm sick . . ." Sally whispered under the blast, and closed her eyes.

"Just hang on," Flynn said, and he wasn't sure whether he was talking to Sally or himself.

Forget about silly little sails, and catching fish and waving at ships; this is what it is all about. Stay on the crate and keep Sally with you tonight, and just maybe you will see tomorrow. It is that simple.

God I'm scared.

The sea became deeper and wilder. The sky rumbled and caught subdued gleams of light behind immense shadows, giving Flynn flickering glimpses of a heaving black ocean. An ocean fit for huge battleships, never for a tiny water-logged crate. The crate was no longer bouncing about on a choppy sea, but sliding into dark valleys and pitching over wind-streaked ridges. Flynn and Sally were trying to keep the crate stable by moving their weight about, but they were becoming very tired.

And then there was a boom. A heavy crash over the sound of the wind and the water.

"What's that?" Sally sounded weak.

"I don't know." Flynn searched for something to cling to. "Perhaps it's waves on a beach."

Another boom, a long roll of thunder, closer and louder. Flynn sat up and was nearly pitched from the crate by a rolling swell. He peered out into the sea and tried to make something out of a mass of waves that jostled, dipped and reared but seemed to be going nowhere at all.

"I can't see . . . Oh!"

It was as if the sea was suddenly ripped open, this time with a crack instead of a boom. Before Flynn the water was torn by a white line of foam that hung in the air before it spread and died. The slash of foam had covered forty meters in three seconds and had disappeared as suddenly as it had occurred.

Bumbora.

Flynn had heard the word in the Lavers' living room. It meant a submerged reef of rock, only visible in low tide or when a heavy sea crashed down upon it. The crate was thirty meters from this bumbora and was being driven towards the center of it by the waves.

"What is it. Is it a monster?" Sally stared, wide-eyed, at where the white foam had been.

"No. A reef."

A long wave before them humped and cracked open with a splintering explosion. The sea seemed to be gasping with the impact and trails of flat foam ran out to the black water. The crate was running downhill towards the reef.

And all Flynn could do was sit on the crate and watch himself sliding into the bumbora and think: there's nothing I can do, there's nothing I can do . . .

A wave tilted the crate, sliding under it, sped away and hurled itself onto a long, gleaming black rock fifteen meters away.

Flynn was shouting at Sally but he could not hear the sound of his own voice through the roar and the crash and he could not remember what he was trying to say, so he just yelled.

Another wave humped under the crate and a rock appeared in the swirling water before and below Flynn's feet. Somewhere a cat was screaming. Flynn lifted his feet and the crate tobogganed towards the rock. A cannon was fired in Flynn's ear and he closed his eyes.

The crate hit something solid and skewed, and stopped. The water roared over the top of the crate and Flynn was underwater for several seconds, clutching at planks and Sally. Another explosion and the crate was twisting and bobbing and free. Flynn shook his head, even had time to grin at Sally.

Then a wave surged under the crate and pushed it into the sky. And the sky cracked, a jagged shaft of light forking and forking across the cloud, shattering the night like a stone through a windshield. For a moment they were sitting on a hill of water above an ocean pouring in confusion around that black reef.

"We made it!" Flynn shouted. "We're still going!"

A moment later the crate tilted and began to slide into a black pit. Flynn saw the wall of water barrel towards him and reached for Sally.

He was hit by something warm, wet and immense. And suddenly there was no wind, no Sally, no crate, nothing at all.

FLYNN surfaced and realized that he was on his own, that the crate was twisting away with nobody on board. He started to chase the crate, his throat choked in panic, then realized that Sally must be here in the water beside him, and stopped.

"Sally!" The word was ripped from his throat.

No answer and the box was climbing a swell away from him.

Catch the crate, then look for Sally . . .

"Sally! Hooey!" He swallowed a mouthful of water.

Somebody was coughing. Behind him.

He turned and saw a black shape on the dark water, and seized a very nearly submerged Sally by the hair. He kicked very hard in the direction he had seen the crate.

No, he couldn't see the crate, he was too tired and Sally wasn't saying anything. This is the end.

Something solid a wave away.

Disappeared. No, in a trough. Must catch it before a wave and the wind gets behind it. Never see it then.

Kicking so hard, using his free arm to pull his body

through the water, but his legs were lead, he wanted to let go and he kept swallowing waves.

The crate has gone, it's sunk . . .

A swell lifted Flynn and Sally and cascaded them behind the crate, now rising to the wind.

Flynn clutched at the crate, bit the wood, hurled Sally on board and was rolled over it by a breaking wave. Made it!

The crate was showing a different side, the bucket gone, the cat gone, but Sally was coughing out water.

She opened her eyes. "Where's Nebu?" she said when she could fill her lungs with air.

"Take it easy." The fear was going down now, but he was feeling incredibly weak.

Lightning cracked across the sky, catching Sally's white face as she screamed and the shape of something black pulling itself onto the crate. It opened its mouth and the sea shook with thunder. It bared its fangs and hissed as its angular, dripping body coiled onto the boards.

"Ruddy cat," said Flynn, and felt strangely like laughing.

Flynn and Sally coughed at each other for another minute and Nebu tolerated Sally scratching him.

Then it rained.

It poured. As if someone had unzipped the clouds. There was so much water in the air Flynn wasn't sure where the sea began. But the rain was almost warm, it beat the waves down and the wind seemed to be dropping. The air was hissing.

Flynn reached across and shook Sally's shoulder. "Drink it," he said.

"What?"

Flynn demonstrated. He lay back on the crate and opened his mouth. He had to close his eyes, and then throw his arm over them to protect them from the battering of the rain. The inside of his mouth became a little numb but filled. He swallowed, said, "See?" and filled again.

Funny that the rain should taste of salt. But it wasn't as salty as the sea and there was nothing he could do about it. Funny, too, that he should be as cold as he was and be as thirsty as he was at the same time.

Sally tried drinking water like her brother, then cupped her hands and drank from them as from a bowl. She lowered her hands for Nebu.

When the rain stopped the waves increased a little, but they were nowhere as bad as they had been. Sally and Flynn lay on the box with Nebu between them, and shivered until they were too tired to shiver.

Flynn began to feel warm, cozy and drowsy. He smiled and released his grip on the edges to sprawl, lolling as the crate rocked him. Then one corner of his mind remembered something and kicked the rest of him awake. If you sleep when you're very cold you just never wake up. He'd read that somewhere.

"Sally . . ." He shoved the girl's shoulder. Sally shrugged and kept her eyes closed. "C'mon, Sally."

One eye opened. "Are we there?"

"No. You've got to sit up."

"Why?"

"Because." Flynn had thought briefly of telling Sally there was a magic mermaid they had to watch for, but that had all changed. "Because it's too cold to go to sleep. We have to get warm. Sit up."

The waves had softened to a long roll and the wind faded to a breeze. Flynn sat opposite Sally and shook the weariness from his head.

"We'll do the little pigs." Flynn raised a finger.

"We did it."

"When?"

"This morning."

"Ah." That long ago? A year ago, a century. "Oh, yes."

"We'll do Pat-a-cake." She held her hands up.

"Patty cake, patty—" He smacked her hands.

Sally pulled her hands away and sighed. "You're still doing it wrong. Pat-a-cake, pat-a-cake, baker's man . . . ," spanking his hands slowly and deliberately.

"Faster."

"PatitandprickitandmarkitwithT!" Sally's hands began to glow red and a touch of mischief crept across her face. "Putitintheoven for Flynny and me!"

"Yeah. Hey diddle diddle . . ."

It was a very long night. They repeated everything they had recited and sung in the morning and played I Can See with My Little Eye in Dad's Sitting Room because they could not see at all. That game petered out after some disagreement over what was in the sitting room and because it had a sad and hollow ring to it. In the end they just talked enough to keep each other awake.

And very slowly the rolling sea flattened and the breeze died, leaving the crate motionless on a dark glass plate.

"Sally . . . ?"

"Mmm?" Sally said reluctantly after a long time.

"Do you like to remember the farm?"

"A bit."

"I was thinking about it. We shouldn't have left." Sally stroked Nebu.

"It was a good place, wasn't it? Dad shouldn't have dragged us all into the city. Should he?"

"I didn't like the farm much."

Nebu uncoiled slowly and walked to the edge of the crate.

"Why? There was everything, all the bush trails, the wild animals, the wallabies, lizards . . ."

"I never saw a wallaby."

"Oh, that was early on. They'd come back with the rain. And there's Guinnigan's Hole . . ."

"Yeuch. Just a place full of black mud and bugs. Boys like funny things."

"It *was* good. Even girls would go there. When it had water."

"And I didn't like the dead sheep . . . Nebu!"

Nebu very gracefully stepped off the crate.

Sally cried out and frantically clutched at the empty air where the cat had been.

Flynn heard the splash and moved his head slightly. "What's up?"

Sally peered at the black water and held her hand above the planks, still feeling the fur on her fingers. "Nebu!" She shouted several times, petering to a bare whisper. "Nebu . . . he's gone."

Her shoulders began to shake, her back arched forward, her throat moved in spasms. She began to cry.

This time Flynn did not try to stop her. He looked at her distantly and began to remember.

SIXTEEN

FLYNN had gone to bed early that night. No. Flynn had been sent to bed early that night. Sent to join Sally and to get him out of the way. For weeks Dad and Mum had been acting strangely, looking at each other as if they had stolen something, walking about with almost nothing to do, and whispering a lot. Dad seemed to give up work on the farm and he spent many days driving off somewhere in his truck, returning only at night. Every day he was a little more tired.

Three days ago Ewen's dad drove his dusty Chevy up to the farm, talked a lot with Dad and walked around all morning. He would point his knobbly walking stick at a sheep, wave the stick at another and prod at a hard clod when Dad talked. After a while he shrugged, wrote something, gave Dad a scrap of paper, shrugged again and drove away.

After that Dad kept the sheep in two paddocks. Most of them were herded into the dusty top paddock away from the house. Some of them had to be carried into the paddock, they were that weak. The others were allowed into the stubble of the failed wheat and left free to roam.

And tonight Flynn sprawled under a sheet in the stifling dark and listened to the house creak. He knew there was something terribly wrong but he did not know what it was and anyway Dad would fix it. After a while he could hear the voices of Mum and Dad as a subdued murmur through two walls. If he concentrated very hard he could make out what they were saying. Dad was taking something long and heavy from the top of a wardrobe.

". . . there's nothing else, is there?" Mum's voice, strangely uneven and very tired.

"No. That's it."

"Oh, what a waste."

"Harry's taking all he can bear. Just the ones he reckons might last a bit. Good bloke, Harry." Dad was taking a box that clinked a little from a drawer.

"And there's no other farm."

"They'll be following us."

"Well, we tried . . ."

"Look . . . See you later." Dad walked to the door and closed it quietly behind him.

An hour later the shooting started.

FLYNN sat alone on the crate and waited for the sky to lighten. Sally had cried herself to sleep and now was breathing slowly and deeply beside him.

She's thinking of home, he thought. And for her

home means Bankstown. For me, it's the farm and I can't go home.

Why, why, why. Why?

"WHY?"

Dad stared down at Flynn with the rising sun at his back. "Because we have to, that's why. Because we are finished here. We have to start again at some other place."

"But I like it here. All my friends are here. I know everything here." Flynn was blinking water from his eyes.

"Do you think we want to leave? We just have to, that's all. We tried but the drought beat us. It happens. Now give your mother a hand with the packing."

"But it's our farm! Why do we have to leave?"

"It's not our farm anymore."

"It's not fair."

Dad's face darkened and for the first time in Flynn's life he saw Dad's hands become fists. Mum bustled Flynn into another room and made him help her with a carton.

"It's not so bad, really," Mum said brightly. "We're going to Sydney and everything will be new and different."

"I don't want it to be different."

"You're not trying, Flynn. Don't you want to go surfing, or sailing, watch rugby league? Ah, there are five television stations in Sydney, hundreds of movie theaters, the zoo . . .'' But her cheeks were wet.

"No. I want to stay here."

When the packing was done and the old truck loaded enough to flatten its springs, Flynn was almost thrown into the cabin. He was complaining about needing time to say good-bye to all his friends.

And Dad found a single shell in his pocket. He tossed it in the air, caught it and reached for the gun.

Flynn shut up.

"What are you doing?" Mum called, with Sally riding her hip.

Dad rammed the shell into the rifle without a word, aimed at the white furnace of the sun and fired.

"That didn't do much good," said Mum.

"I feel a little better. Now let's go." He drove the truck down the corrugated track without looking back.

ALL the way to Bankstown with a whining kid on his neck, Flynn thought as he stared at the black sea.

He's got to start from scratch in a different life. He's got to forget about sheep and farming and learn all about accountancy at the same time as he's working for money for us to live on. Mum's all the way behind him. Sally's never any trouble, but good ol' Flynn always wants things that aren't there anymore. It's not that Dad has changed. It's that everything has changed except you and you keep wanting it all back.

Now why didn't you think of that before?

Doesn't matter. This time, if we get . . .

If.

Flynn noticed a change in the sky. Just a shift in the black.

And he realized that the sun that Dad had shot at could show him that he was going to die. He knuckled at the wood before him as his stomach twisted.

If the morning light showed him nothing but a great circle of sea that would be it. Yesterday's sunburn would deepen into blisters and there would be no water. Sally would not last past the afternoon and he would have killed her with his bloody stupid pirate game. If he was lucky then he'd die before night.

He closed his eyes and rubbed them until fiery globes soared across the inside of his lids.

A line. Maybe a line.

Why did that cat jump? Maybe it got too cold and wet and tired and scared to go on. Maybe it just didn't know what it was doing. Or, maybe it knew . . .

Definitely a line forming now out in the sea. Black on black, but the top black wasn't quite as black as the bottom black.

It is too low.

Flynn felt something die in him. He looked for another line, a high bumpy line, something like a hill or a cliff, in the dark sky, but there was nothing. He tried to persuade himself that the low line was higher than it was, that he had lost his balance in a storm, that the line wasn't really straight, it had a couple of small dunes along its length . . .

It was no good. The line was low and straight. It could only be the horizon of a calm sea. The current had carried them out again.

What do you tell Sally now?

Nothing. She'll know. When she wakes she'll know.

Flynn watched the horizon for a while. He wanted to shout at it as Dad had fired at the sun, but that might wake Sally. He didn't want to wake Sally for a long, long time.

He eased himself back and stared at the sky over his head, darker than the horizon. He watched the sky slowly wash to dark gray and felt his body come to life. He was shivering and his skin chafed under his wet, torn shirt, his muscles ached and his face, his neck, his lips began to burn. When the sun came up and the clouds drifted away the sun was going to fry them like bacon.

He inflated his cheeks and hissed sadly at the brightening horizon.

At least they had tried. Like Dad and Mum on that farm they'd put everything they had into it. Flynn remembered trying to push the crate back to shore, and Sally screaming with Nebu in her hair, the fishing, the ship, the shark, the sail, the storm, the bumbora, the capsize. They'd tried so hard, but like Dad they failed.

And just when he'd just got to understand Dad. Or maybe just got to understand a bit of himself . . .

The sun should not be rising there.

He jerked himself up and turned. He trembled, felt astonishingly weak. He palmed his eyes and began to giggle.

Through the night Flynn and Sally had sat on the crate facing one way with the wind and waves behind them and that single glimpse of land vaguely in front of them. But the wind and the waves had slipped away and the clouds had obliterated the stars. Naturally the crate had turned in many circles but Flynn had been too tired to work that out. He had accepted as certain fact that his sprawled legs were pointing towards the land they had left so long ago. In fact the place where Flynn had thought the sun had set was going to play host to the rising sun.

"Stupid," Flynn said kindly. "Very, very stoopid."

Over his shoulder there was a different horizon, black under a very dark gray. This horizon was very high, and it wasn't straight at all, it had bumps, hollows, crevasses . . .

"Sally." Flynn touched his sister on the arm.

"Mmn . . ."

Gray sky with a little shadow, spikes on the horizon.

Spikes? Sword grass on cliffs or sand dunes. That close? "Sally. Wake up."

"Go 'way."

"I'll leave you here."

Sally sat up with eyes closed.

A long sandy beach was sliding from the gloom. No more than thirty meters away.

Flynn turned her head. "Now look."

"Oh," Sally said, still drowsy. "We're there."

"I'll tow us in." Flynn leapt from the crate, landed with a splash and began to laugh.

Sally frowned at him. "What's wrong?"

Flynn stopped laughing. He kicked his feet under him and rose from the water until it lapped about his waist. He held out his hands to her. "C'mon. Let's go ashore."

Sally took his hands and jumped into the water. She felt the sand between her toes and tried to run towards the beach, clawing at the water beneath her armpits and bobbing wildly. Flynn let her go.

He patted the crate, almost affectionately, and staggered slowly towards the quiet shore, listening to the long ripples in the wet sand and trying to remember how to walk. He could not convince himself that the bar beneath his feet was not rocking a little. Or that it was all over.

Then Sally shouted from the shallows and splashed very fast onto the beach and Flynn thought, Shark!

He ran, his knees hurling spray in arcs before him. When he reached the dry sand he toppled sideways with a grateful sigh.

Ahead, Sally was crouched on all fours. She was saying, "Poor little thing, poor wet little thing," as if she was talking to a baby.

Nebu ignored her and licked his paw.

Flynn sighed and closed his eyes.

FLYNN woke to hear Sally shouting and dancing as a sleek boat of chrome and fiberglass nosed towards the beach. He climbed unsteadily to his feet, brushed sand from his body and looked at the crate as it drifted out to sea.

He felt strange.

He frowned at the gently bobbing crate and said, "Avast there," very quietly.

No. Somehow that wasn't him anymore.

He watched the boat with a sudden dead feeling in his stomach. The next few days were going to be very bad, with Dad, Mum, Norm, even the police tearing strips off him. He didn't want to go through that.

Flynn hesitated and thought of Dad towering over him, saying: "Why, boy, why did you do it? It was the stupidest thing I have ever heard of! And with tiny little Sal. You almost killed her, you know that, don't you . . ." And Flynn thought of turning from the boat and running through the rocks to the trees and safety. He would become the last of the bush-rangers . . .

But only for a moment. He knew he would have to take it all. There really was no option. The thing that astonished him was that now he knew that he *could* take it. And maybe after it was all over he and Dad could be mates again . . .

Flynn stepped from the seventeenth-century sea-boots, picked up the cat and strode towards the boat.